ONE WAY TRIP

STEPHEN M. BRAUND

This is a work of fiction. Names, characters, businesses, places, events and incidents are either the products of the author's imagination or used in a fictitious manner. Any resemblance to actual persons, living or dead, or actual events is purely coincidental.

Editors: Jesse Scoble and Suzanne Hartwick

Cover Art: Nicolas Gardeazabal

Author Photo: John Anthony

ISBN: 0993864422
ISBN-13: 978-0993864421

First Edition

For Christine, Tyler, and Brody.
Your love keeps me Earth-bound.

CONTENTS

ACKNOWLEDGMENTS

Writing can sometimes feel as lonely as a one way trip to Mars. It's easy to get lost along the way without guidance from mission control. For a writer, working with a great editor is the embodiment of this, helping to navigate though an infinite combination of words, grammar and punctuation. With this book, I was lucky enough to work with two editors.

The first, Jesse Scoble, I also have the privilege of calling a friend. His ruthless slaughter of weak adverbs, prolific semi-colons, and other hidden darlings has helped shape and guide several of my stories, including this one.

I was also fortunate to work for the first time with Suzanne Hartwick, who brought a fresh perspective to the story (along with her sharp red pen) which led to the birth of a few new scenes and greater depth for several characters.

For the cover artwork, I was thrilled to enlist the talents of Nicolas Gardeazabal (ngillustration.com). His work is so extraordinary, I actually hope people judge this book by its cover.

To all of them—and to my other readers, writing friends, and the whole supportive writing community I've connected with on Twitter—I would like to say thank you. You've all helped bring this book to life.

-S.

PROLOGUE

Earth, 2025

I close my eyes at the deafening explosion of the rocket engines. The force of the 70 tonne bomb beneath me jams my spine into the seat as it fights gravity and lifts its mammoth weight into the sky. At the same time, a blast of adrenaline rips through my nervous system, making my heart pound so hard I can feel my head throbbing. With each breath, I feel the gnawing fear that it may be my last.

Nine minutes.

From liftoff to orbit it takes nine minutes. But during those nine minutes my senses will be assaulted by the violence of the rocket beneath me, ripping itself free from the planet's grip.

I remind myself that this is a dream come true, that after all my years of training I am finally on my way into space. All I have to do is survive the next nine minutes and it will all be worth it.

Everything is shaking, but I try to watch the panel of sensors in front of me for any indication of a problem. There may only be a split second to jettison the capsule clear of the rocket before a catastrophic failure.

I can only hope I'll get a chance to react. But another voice tells me I'll be incinerated before I realize it.

So much for staying calm and focused.

My stomach twists into a tighter knot despite my pre-launch dose of anti-nausea drugs. I find it hard to breathe, and I know it's from more than just the tremendous g-forces crushing my chest. The panic no longer lurks in the back of my mind, it's kicking the door down.

I have to try another tactic; something to calm me. I need to find a happy memory to shut out all the noise and confusion, a time when the calm outweighed the chaos.

But then, I already know which memory to choose, because it's always been the same one.

The day I met *her*.

CHAPTER 1

Earth, 1999

The most precious thing in the world isn't gold or diamonds, it's the innocence with which a child views the world. We only ever get it once in our lifetime, and without ever realizing its value, it becomes lost to us forever.

Mine was shattered at the age of five when my father and little brother died in a car accident. I remember with absolute clarity my mother crying so hard she couldn't tell me what was wrong. I had never seen my mother cry before, so I began crying too. Even when she got the words out, I didn't understand that I would never see my dad and little brother ever again—until I saw their matching coffins at the funeral. Then it hit home. The memory of my life began with the accident, and everything before it was a blur. I can't even remember their faces.

Looking back, I think a part of my mother died that day too; I just didn't realize it then. What I did realize was that she was smoking—a lot. And sometimes when she smoked I would see a haunted look in her eyes. I dreaded that look. It was like she was staring at ghosts.

And while she stared them down, she was chain-smoking her way on an express train to join them.

When she focused on the living, my mother smothered me with every kindness she could think of. She spoiled me enough for two sons, and it felt good to receive that much attention. We were two willing accomplices, allowing each other to numb our grief.

By the time I turned nine, my sense of entitlement knew no bounds. If I wanted something, I had to have it, and my mother's feelings were of little consequence to me. If she showed even the slightest hesitation to a request, I piled on the guilt, like pressing a thumb into a festering wound. So what if it made her smoke through that next carton a little faster? The important thing was that I got what I wanted.

When my latest whim was for an expensive telescope, I already knew later that night I would be staring up at the stars. But just peering at them through my bedroom window wasn't enough; my nine-year-old brain insisted I had to have an open sky overhead for an awesome astrological experience.

Although I could easily extort my mother for playthings, she was unyielding when it came to my safety. So if I wanted to go out alone to the playground on a cold winter's night to set up my telescope, I would need to sneak out.

And so that night, after my mother tucked me into bed and said goodnight, I grabbed my jacket from under my bed, folded up the telescope, and climbed out my window. After a short trek, I set up my makeshift observatory atop the jungle gym in the darkened playground.

I had just discovered the Big Dipper when I heard voices approaching in the darkness. From the cracking vocal chords and snippets of swear words, I knew there were at least two older boys wandering my way. I froze, hoping they wouldn't notice me, but the plume of frost from my silhouette betrayed me.

I saw them stop as they spotted me. One was big and round with a square head. The other one was small and thin, with a ball cap turned sideways to look cool, though it had the opposite effect.

"What'cha doing up there, dickwad?" Square Head called out.

"Nothing," was my clever reply.

The high pitch of my grade school voice was like meat dangling in front of a pair of Dobermans. In a flash the two of them scaled the jungle gym and surrounded me. They smelled like they hung out in the same ashtray as my mother.

"You lookin' for aliens or something?"

"I think he's looking in people's windows, like some sicko little perv!" Side Cap said.

My heart was hammering in my ears, but I didn't look up and I didn't reply. I was afraid of looking afraid.

"Yo, we're talking to you…!" Square Head said, stepping closer until I was crushed between them. I felt the heat of their breath on my face.

"Leave him alone."

The girl's voice out of the darkness surprised me. It had a similar effect on the bullies as they both took a step back.

"Piss off, Gwen," Square Head said.

"Yeah," the other one added. "We're just having fun."

I couldn't see the girl, but I could hear she had moved closer.

"I don't think he'd call it having fun," she said. "Marco, what do you think mom would say if she heard you were out here picking on little kids? After those letters from school, I don't she'd be very happy. She might even tell dad."

"Why do you always have to be such a little bitch?!" said Marco Square Head.

"Yeah, you're a real bitch, *Pen Gwen*!" added Side Cap. In case she missed his clever play on words, he did a little waddle and made a quacking sound that no penguin in existence had ever made.

"That's really funny Fred," Gwen said to Side Cap, "because I heard you have a nickname too—*Freddy Bedwetty*."

I liked the name Freddy Bedwetty *much* better than Side Cap.

"Shut up!" yelled Freddy Bedwetty.

"Why don't you make me?" asked Gwen. "Come on, I can't wait to hear you explain to all your friends tomorrow how you got beat up by a girl."

Silence followed as a standoff was reached. I tried not to breathe, hoping they'd forget about me.

"You're a bitch!" repeated Freddy Bedwetty.

"I know. You both said that already," Gwen replied.

It was Marco Square Head who finally decided to end it.

"Fine," he said. "If you love the little geek so much, you can have him!"

With that, he gave me and my telescope a quick shove off the jungle gym.

Before I knew it, the ground slammed into me and crushed the air from my lungs. I lay there unable to get up, half-buried in a snow bank; it felt like both Marco Square Head and Freddy Bedwetty were sitting on my chest.

But the two bullies were already walking away, snorting with laughter at their superiority.

"Are you all right?" she asked.

I looked up and saw my savior emerge like an angel out of the darkness.

She looked like she was only a couple of years older than me, with wisps of blond hair flowing out of a knit cap. She was bundled up in a bulky winter jacket and scarf, but I thought she was the most beautiful girl I had ever seen.

"Can't…" I gasped.

"You just got winded from the fall," she said as she kneeled down beside me. "Try to relax and breathe. You'll be okay in a minute."

Up close she was even more beautiful, from the rounded curve of her nose, to the pillowed shape of her lips and the light flutter of her eyelashes, I found myself noticing things I had never noticed about a girl before. If the ground hadn't beaten her to the punch, she would have taken my breath away.

"What's your name?" Gwen asked.

"Martin," I squeaked, as my lungs slowly started sucking in the cold winter air.

"I'm Gwen," she said. "I'm sorry my brother and his friend are such jerks."

"He's really your brother?" I asked, slowly getting to my feet.

"I know. I don't know how we could be related either."

"Thank you… for what you did."

"Did they break your telescope?" Gwen asked.

I had nearly forgotten all about it. It lay in the snow only a few feet away. Once I was able to get back on my feet I picked it up and brushed the snow away from the lens, looking for cracks.

"Don't think so," I said. "Let's see…"

I hooked the telescope and tripod under my arm and climbed back to the top of the jungle gym. Once it was set up, I peered into the viewfinder and saw the panorama of stars.

"It works!" I laughed.

"Can I look?" Gwen asked. She was suddenly next to me and I jumped so much I had to catch myself from falling off the jungle gym again.

"Uh, sure," I said, hoping my red face wasn't glowing in the dark. "Go ahead."

Gwen put her eye to the viewfinder and her lips curved into a smile.

"Beautiful," she said.

"Yeah," I agreed.

"I want to go up there someday," Gwen said.

"Really?"

"Yeah," she looked over at me. "You?"

"Sure." I shrugged. "That would be cool."

Truthfully, I had not even thought about it until that moment. But now the idea of being an astronaut seemed like the coolest thing in the world.

To highlight the perfection of the moment, large flakes of snow began to float down all around us, even though when I looked up, I couldn't see any clouds in the sky.

"Wow, look at that!" Gwen said. "It's like a million little stars are falling from the sky!"

She threw her head back and stuck out her tongue, hopping back and forth trying to catch a snowflake. Her laugh was infectious, and after a moment I also had my tongue out, trying to catch snowflakes. What fragments remained of my childhood innocence prevented any thought of doing something brash.

It felt like we were chasing snowflakes with our tongues forever, when Gwen finally turned back to me.

"Well I guess I'd better catch up to my big dopey brother," she said. "He's an idiot, but he's not stupid enough to show up at home without me. You live around here too?"

"Yeah," I said, hiking a thumb over my shoulder, "just over that way."

"Funny, I never noticed you before," she replied. "Guess I'll be seeing you around."

"For sure!" I said, a little too enthusiastically.

She laughed. "Goodbye, Martin."

"Goodbye, Gwen."

And with that, she scaled down the jungle gym and faded back into the darkness.

As if on cue, the snow stopped. I just stood there, staring after her.

I wasn't feeling the cold at all.

CHAPTER 2

Earth orbit, 2025

M artin."

A hand touching my shoulder snaps me out of my daydream. In the seat next to me, Jomo—my "space-brother-from-another-mother"—smiles. The blue sky outside our cockpit has melted away into a black velvet curtain hung with countless shimmering diamonds. Peering up at the stars through a telescope cannot compare to the astonishing beauty here among them.

There's a jolt as the last stage of our rocket drops away to burn up in the atmosphere. My eyes snap to the mission clock.

Nine minutes and twenty seconds.

Mission Control confirms that we have optimal trajectory as we begin our orbit of Earth. The cockpit slowly rotates, and the stars slide away to reveal the most extraordinary sight.

The dull ache in my jaw reminds me that I can unclench my teeth, but my mouth has already dropped open in awe.

It's so *beautiful.*

The stars may be stunning, but the Earth below us is magnificent. It is both awe-inspiring and heartbreaking. The lifetime I spent anchored to the trivialities on the surface had seemed so easy to give up. But looking down at this beautiful blue marble, with only a thin haze of atmosphere above to protect it, I can see how fragile the planet is, and how perfect. It strikes me that I've made a terrible mistake. Knowing this realization is already years too late makes it that much more gut-wrenching.

My vision blurs as tears fill my eyes, but they have nowhere to go in zero gravity. I have to take several deep breaths and keep blinking to squeeze the tears onto my eyelashes. I look back at Jomo and see his eyes are as wet as mine.

"It's so beautiful," Jomo says. "What were we thinking?"

I can only shrug and shake my head.

I wrench my eyes away and try to focus on the stars ahead. I need to remember why I decided to do this in the first place. Right now there is no time for regrets; if I'm lucky, I'll live long enough to regret this later.

After a few quick spins around the globe, the final rocket stage will fire us out of orbit and onwards towards our destination.

Mars.

Out of the billions of people below, Jomo and I earned the honor of being the first to go. We each had our own unique qualifications—training and aptitude atop the list. But there was one other thing required from each astronaut for this particular trip, something which allowed us to step in for the usual crew cuts with all their "Right Stuff".

After seven months of hurtling through space towards Mars, our tiny capsule will land on the red planet with no way to get us back off of the surface. We will be making Mars our new home.

This is what we signed up for.

A one way trip.

Once upon a time, the glory of space exploration was the exclusive domain of governments. But massive worldwide debts sapped political hunger, even as dreams of interstellar travel still whetted the public's appetite. The corporations became the natural successors to the space race. With politics out of the way, multinational conglomerates consolidated and crafted a business plan to achieve the holy grail of space exploration: landing humans on Mars.

But every business has investors, and those investors didn't like waiting forever for a return on their investment. While the conglomerates had all the technology they needed to land on Mars, the inevitable roadblock was getting the astronauts home. An atomic power source was the only thing both small and powerful enough to transport to Mars and then use for the return launch, but nations were united in their opposition to sending nuclear rockets into the sky that weren't meant to incinerate their enemies.

That's when the board of directors came up with a simple solution: don't bring the astronauts back. Instead of just visiting Mars, they would colonize it. They could start sending out teams of astronauts to Mars within the decade without having to spend billions upfront in research and development. This was the sort of timeline that could be profitable. The investors were delighted.

All they had to do was find some volunteers willing to give up everything. Volunteers willing to forgo the comforts of a lush, populated planet equipped to sustain life, for a lonely and barren planet, whose only promise would be never-ending pursuit of new ways to kill you.

In a testament to the human spirit, people all over the world volunteered, numbering in the millions.

From those many millions, Jomo and I are the first to make the trip.

A new countdown begins, and moments later the rumbling engines vibrate my weightless flesh in waves. Compared to the rocket's soul-shaking blast at launch, this smaller final stage is practically an amusement ride as we accelerate away from the Earth's gravitational pull. It's an eerie feeling as the bright blue glow behind us dims to black. We have no choice but to focus on the twinkling red ruby among the black sea of stars.

As the firing rockets die out, a small concussion wave marks the final stage dropping away from our capsule to become another floating scrap of space junk. Then we deploy our solar arrays, which will track the sun's position and keep our capsule powered for the duration of the voyage.

This final push should be enough momentum for the next seven months, as we thread the needle towards our target. A more accurate analogy would be that our capsule is attempting to leap between two moving cars speeding around different-sized elliptical tracks, with a little over 50 million kilometers between each car. But this isn't a straight line jump; by the time we catch up to Mars' orbit, we'll have logged well over 711 million kilometers.

"Mission Control to Mars Alpha," the radio crackles, "Everything checks off good and green."

We hear the cheers from our send-off party over the static. Jomo unclips his helmet and pulls it off, inhaling a deep breath of our carbon dioxide-scrubbed air.

"Now the fun begins!" Jomo says, spinning his helmet in a pirouette across our cramped cabin.

Cool.

In all the commotion of leaving Earth behind, I almost forgot that we are now weightless. I remove my own helmet and take a nervous breath.

"Oh yeah? Watch this!" I try to spin my helmet on my finger like a basketball. But the touch of my finger sends it careening off across the cabin, just missing the control panel.

"Maybe after seven months of practice you'll get better at it," Jomo jokes.

"Don't count on it," I reply.

It's time to settle in for what's ahead. Despite spending the last two years in close quarters training with Jomo, nothing quite compares to this. For the better part of the next year our entire shared living space is the equivalent of a small room inside the smallest New York City apartment.

The cramped quarters lead to another thought crossing my mind. I try to shake it, but the thought lingers, and sends a chill up my spine.

It feels like being in a coffin.

CHAPTER 3

Earth, 2002

I stared at my mother lying in her coffin, expecting her to turn her head and tell me to stop crying. But she was too still—an unnatural figure molded in wax. The open casket was courtesy of my Aunt Martha's dogmatic obedience to Catholic tradition. Saying goodbye to a pair of lacquer coffins at my father and brother's funeral hadn't felt nearly as traumatic.

My mother's death created a black hole in my universe. I was twelve years old and an orphan, trapped somewhere between an angry child and an angst-ridden teenager. For six long months I watched the cancer eat away at her. Each passing day both of us grew more terrified of a future without her. I couldn't eat or sleep and I soon began to mirror my mother's gaunt and stricken pallor.

I owe my survival during that time to Gwen. She would appear at our door every week and stay until she had found some way to help us. Sometimes it was helping with the household chores, or bringing food and convincing us to eat. When either one of us broke down into tears it was Gwen who listened, never flinching.

I began to understand why Gwen spent so much time with us and avoided going home. She rarely mentioned her father, but when she did, the fear in her voice was unmistakable. Gwen's mother encouraged her to spend more time with us, yet I could tell there were times when Gwen felt guilty for being away from her mother for so long. Gwen even worried for her brother, Marco. Although I couldn't empathize, her concern for him alarmed me. If she was worried about her brother's safety, then just how dangerous was her father?

But each time I offered to listen, she would laugh it off. I should have insisted, but I was afraid prying too hard might push Gwen away.

My mother never pressed me about my friendship with Gwen, although I doubt it was hard for her to read my true feelings. I think it comforted her knowing someone was there looking out for me. Perhaps that was why my mother opened our door and accepted Gwen's help.

I had no idea if Gwen had any feelings for me. She was my best friend—in truth my only friend—and that made me feel lucky. I wasn't about to mess with a good thing asking a question for which I probably didn't want the answer.

That final week in the hospital was an absolute horror. My mother was so heavily sedated she just lay there with her jaw drooped open, gasping for air with a mechanical rhythm. I sat by her bedside as her life ebbed away day after day, the end ticking closer with each passing moment.

Sometimes a visitor would float through, ask how I was doing, and then evaporate back into the real world the moment the unbearable revulsion overwhelmed them.

Gwen was different. She came every day and sat with me for hours, holding my hand. She smiled and talked to my mother and did her best to add some life to a room where it had been sucked out. I was in the darkest place of my life, yet Gwen was like a beacon of light, constant, keeping me from becoming lost.

And when that final labored breath came, my mother's pale skin turning sallow to the monotone tune of the flat-lining monitors, it was Gwen's shoulder I cried on, clinging to her with whatever remaining shreds of strength she had afforded me.

The few days between my mother's passing and the funeral flew by in a blur. My Aunt Martha swooped in from Montreal to take over; I remembered meeting her and my uncle Alain only a couple of times before. She looked nothing like my mother, and she certainly didn't share my mom's free spirit. Although not unkind, her direct and rigid approach to life sent cultural shockwaves through a kid used to a much more bohemian lifestyle.

And then there I stood, staring at the mortician's rigid rendering of my mother as she lay in her coffin. My head pounded, partly from trying to choke back my emotions, but mostly due to my tie, knotted like a hangman's noose around my neck. I could never understand why funeral parlors were so hot and stuffy when they were meant to display corpses.

A steady stream of people I'd never met drifted by and mumbled their condolences. Some shook my hand. A few others tsked and shook their heads, trying to sum up the tragedy for me in a single syllable.

I kept looking over my shoulder, waiting to see Gwen standing there, waiting for her to lift the oppressive weight in the room that was crushing down on me.

But she never came.

Why? Why not this time? After all the times she had been there for me, missing my mother's funeral meant something was wrong. As the hours ticked by and she still didn't show, a new sense of dread knotted in my stomach.

As the clock rounded the last quarter hour I knew for certain she wouldn't be coming. But by then I knew what I had to do.

I mumbled something incoherent to my aunt and uncle about feeling sick, and before they could respond, I slipped out of the room. I went right past the washroom and out the front door into the cold winter night, not caring if anyone saw me. I ran to catch the bus, and within twenty minutes I had reached my neighborhood, hitting the snow covered sidewalks running as soon as the bus doors opened.

The lights outside Gwen's house were off, but I could see the faint flickering glow of a television through the small window in the front door.

As I pulled myself up the front step gasping for breath, I noticed how unusually loud the TV volume was inside. I couldn't find the doorbell in the darkness, so I just pounded on the storm door. I kept hammering until I saw a shadow lumber across the flickering light.

I stepped back from the door just as the porch lights were thrown on, blinding me. The inner door opened, and the noise from the TV hit the storm door, making the glass shudder.

The large silhouette that filled the doorway was Gwen's father. As I stood there blinking against the dancing embers in my eyes, he just loomed there, watching. Finally, he pushed open the storm door with a meaty hand.

"Don't ya Jesus Witnesses have any good sense, banging on people's doors this late?!" he growled.

We had never met before, so I wasn't surprised he didn't recognize me. It took me a moment to realize my suit had given him the wrong impression.

"I'm not a…" I began, but quickly decided not to correct him. "I'm a friend of Gwen's. Is she home?"

This caught him off-guard, and there was a long moment of silence before he responded.

"Naw, she ain't here."

The reek of booze rolling off him made me gag. My eyes wandered to the hand he was using to hold open the storm door; it was bruised and swollen.

I wanted so badly to be brave, to call him a liar and let him hit me too so I could call the police and have him charged.

"Are you sure?" was the best reply I could muster, trying to look into the house around his bulk.

He shifted himself against the door frame to cut off the house from my prying eyes. "I'm sure. Now piss off!"

He slammed the front door without waiting for a reply and doused the lights.

I stood there stunned, unsure what to do next. Over the din of the TV I heard a female voice, followed by his barked reply. The female voice persisted, but was cut off by a sharp slap, followed by a short cry of pain.

Terrified for Gwen, I stumbled off the front porch and hopped over the snow banks to the house next door.

I rang the doorbell and waited anxiously before I saw the slight flicker of light at the peephole.

"Mrs. Ravenswood! It's me, Gwen's friend Martin!" I waved at the peephole. A moment later I heard the security latches unlock, but her door only opened to the length of the chain.

"Martin?" she asked, still uncertain.

I had met Gwen's elderly neighbor Mrs. Ravenswood several times before. During the summer she could often be found outside tending to her sprawling gardens around the house. She was a widow and didn't have anyone to help, except for Gwen who would lend a hand when she saw her in need. Whenever I stopped by and saw the two of them toiling together, I'd inevitably find myself picking up a shovel, or carrying bags of mulch until I was drenched in sweat.

Mrs. Ravenswood also made her own lemonade. She'd mix up a fresh pitcher and serve us refreshments on the front porch in thanks. As we drank it, she'd ask Gwen about how she was doing. Gwen would always insist that everything was fine, but Mrs. Ravenswood would continue to press in such a way that felt like she had more than a passing concern.

Afterwards when I asked her about it, Gwen would just laugh off Mrs. Ravenswood's uncomfortable questions, saying that she was a sweet old lady who worried too much.

But now I realized Mrs. Ravenswood must have seen or heard more than she had let on. I could only hope her concern meant that she was someone I could turn to for help.

"He's hitting them, Mrs. Ravenswood," I blurted out. "He's drunk right now and he's hitting them. You have to call the police."

There was a brief pause as her door closed for a moment, but then I heard the chain scrape aside. This time her door opened all the way and I could see the look of concern on her face. There were questions she wanted to ask, but once she saw the urgency in my eyes, she didn't hesitate.

"Come inside Martin. I'll get the phone," she said.

We waited together by the front window as the minutes ticked by, peering out through the curtains at any movement. When we finally saw the police cruiser pull up, Mrs. Ravenswood held my arm and begged me to wait inside. She was afraid of what might happen if Gwen's father figured out who had called the police.

Another cruiser pulled up. Now there were muffled shouts coming from next door. Soon after that we saw two cops leading Gwen's father out in handcuffs. He appeared to be going along quietly—until he was placed in the back seat. He started to shout at the officers, kicking the windows. The cops responded by opening the back door and dragged him out into a nearby snow bank. To make sure he didn't get up, one of the cops sat on his back while another handcuffed his ankles and hogtied him. It took all four officers to lift and toss him back into the cruiser.

Just then an ambulance arrived. When I saw that, I forgot the promise I had made to Mrs. Ravenswood and bolted outside. A police officer saw me coming and refused to let me by. I tried to explain that I was the one who called them, but the cop was like a brick wall.

"Please, my friend Gwen is in there," I pleaded. "I just want to know if she's okay."

The cop laid a reassuring hand on my shoulder.

"Kid, there's okay, and then there's being okay. Your friend is okay. But with stuff like this, she ain't *never* gonna *be* okay."

The cryptic wisdom bestowed on me by the Buddha in blue was irritating, but I had no other choice.

So I stood there and waited, my adrenaline pounding in my

ears.

Before long, the paramedics emerged from Gwen's house, rolling a stretcher between them with someone strapped in.

"Gwen!" I shouted as I tried to peer around the cop.

"Martin?" Gwen replied.

I looked past the stretcher and saw Gwen coming out of her house with her brother Marco. As the stretcher rolled past I could see Gwen's mother strapped to it. She was conscious, but her face was bruised and bloody.

"Gwen, are you okay?" I asked. To his credit, the cop stepped aside when he saw Gwen's face light up.

Instead of replying, she ran over and hugged me. Not just some awkward comforting shoulder hug like the ones we had once shared, but a full embrace, crushing me into her. At first I stood there in shock, not knowing what to do. The warmth of her embrace was electric. By the time I had recovered my senses she was letting me go.

"Thank you," she said.

"You would have done the same for me," I replied. "In a lot of ways you already have."

She looked back as her mother was loaded into the ambulance.

"I have to go."

"I know," I replied. "I'll see you later."

"Bye Martin," she said to me as she climbed into the back of the ambulance.

"I'll see you soon."

I wouldn't see Gwen again for almost two decades.

CHAPTER 4

Space, 2025

Travelling through space for over half a year in a tiny metal can using nothing more than momentum has become a waking dream. Repetition blurs into routine, and routine into reflex.

Each "day" I wake in darkness, floating in a calm so peaceful, for a moment I think I've returned to the womb. It's only when I lift my head and feel the straps around my shoulders that I remember where I am. Removing my eye mask and earplugs, bright artificial light and a constant electrical hum greet me as my senses come back online.

I unbuckle the straps anchoring me to the wall and unzip my sleeping cocoon. Then I begin tensing muscles in the different areas of my body, reminding them that they're still needed. I pull myself out of my cocoon and say good morning to Jomo, whose staggered sleep schedule has had him up for several hours already.

"Still on course. So yes, it is a good morning," is Jomo's standard reply. Despite the good news, he never takes his eyes off the readings, as though any dereliction of his duty might cause him to miss something.

I work my way over to our washroom, which is nothing more than a set of suction hoses. With Jomo focused on the star field ahead, I'm able to relax and take care of business. Our waste gets sucked out through the hose, but not flushed out of the capsule. Jettisoning anything with mass would cause a deviation in our course, so our waste is packed away and continues on our journey along with us.

Because of weight restrictions water is in very limited supply, so our urine is also saved. We empty the bags into a machine that filters and distills it so we're able to drink it again. The thing they really don't advertise in the astronaut brochure is how much time you spend drinking your own pee. Fortunately, science has yet to develop a method to make our other waste edible. Although, the plan is to use it as a fertilizer for our horticultural efforts on Mars, so there's always that to look forward to.

After a quick breakfast of freeze-dried rations and flavored powder mixed with recycled pee, it's time for the morning exercise routine. A contraption dubbed the "Martian Muscle Maker" unfolds from the wall. It can be used in various configurations for working on different muscle groups. Since lifting weights in zero gravity is effortless, the machine uses air cylinders and stretching bands for resistance. Each set of muscles need daily stimulation; without the constant pull of gravity they are prone to atrophy. I upload the latest briefings from Mission Control on my tablet and then start working through the exercise regimen. The briefings usually don't take very long to read since little changes from day to day. Often we are tasked with a list of simple experiments, though Jomo and I both know that most are only concocted to help us battle the daily tedium.

I've known Jomo for four years now, the last couple spent in close quarters in the desert, training for our mission in the simulation habitat. Besides having a good distribution of skills between us, part of the reason we were matched together was our combination of personalities. Jomo is a brilliant guy with a fantastic attention to detail, all wrapped in a self-deprecating sense of humor and a laid-back style of command. With my need for order and procedure, and a love of the occasional smartass comment, the two of us hit it off right away. The time in the simulation habitat was not only to train us for the first phase of colonization, but also to see how well the two of us would function together for a long period of time.

The project psychologists validated their salaries with our matchup; Jomo and I not only worked well together, but bonded on a level deeper than friendship. He has become like a brother to me, which, according to my psychological profile, was an amazing feat. I learned later that the report stated I had developed a defense mechanism after the death of my brother preventing me from bonding with any male peer. They said that on a subconscious level, I was afraid of letting anyone replace my little brother.

But Jomo proved them wrong. Maybe it was because he was a couple of years older, and for once I could be the little brother. Or maybe it was because he was just as damaged as I was. Either way, he's worthy of admiration, not just for what he has accomplished, but for how he was able to carry on when most people would have just given up.

Jomo is from a small town just outside of Nakuru, Kenya. He lived there his entire life, became a doctor, married his school sweetheart, and had three beautiful daughters. Then one night when he was working late at the hospital, their home caught fire and his entire life turned to ash.

I've never seen Jomo get emotional, but he told me after the fire—after he buried his wife and daughters in four matching white coffins—every last ounce of his emotions was wrung out of him, enough for a lifetime.

"I thought I might go mad with grief," he said, "I wished I would die of a broken heart, but I did not. I survived."

He knew he could have ended his pain by taking his own life, but he never attempted it. The guilt he felt for not being with his family the night of the fire fed his belief that he deserved to suffer, so he took in all of the raw pain and waited for it to break him.

"Then one day, I woke up and there were no more tears," he told me, "I felt empty, a hollow man of skin and clothes, the world passed me by like pictures on a movie screen."

Jomo left the country and his practice behind, never to return. He travelled to other countries in Africa and volunteered his medical skills in poor villages that rarely saw a doctor.

"It gave me a sense of purpose," he said, "But still I felt like a nomad, always on the move, unable to connect to anyone around me."

The psychologists later told Jomo that this was because he felt the need to run away rather than face his problems. He didn't disagree with them.

When he heard about the candidate requirements for the Mars program, Jomo saw an opportunity to run about as far away as possible. Given the magnitude of what he suffered, I couldn't imagine anyone trying to stop him.

The dangers on this mission are as much mental as they are physical. Tedium is a gateway to depression, and our extreme circumstances aggravate any dark mood. Although Jomo and I emotionally support each other as best we can given our scarred pasts, there's always the danger of us reflecting that darkness at each other like a pair of broken mirrors. There have been a few downward spirals, but each time at least one of us was able to snap out of it to pull the other back up.

The one thing that's always able to lift our spirits is the sight of Mars growing larger in front of us each day. The red planet beckons us closer, and we are eager for its gravitational embrace. The warm red glow fills our tiny capsule more each day, chasing the darkness away.

Our shining red beacon of hope.

CHAPTER 5

Earth, 2016

As I opened my eyes, I felt the light stab needles into my brain. I buried my face into my pillow and pulled the covers over my head, determined to retreat back into unconsciousness until reality stopped being so cruel.

There was movement next to me in bed and I froze, snapping awake.

My mind clawed its way back in time through the haze of memories from the night before.

There had been a company mixer. It had been a rough week and I had felt the need to let loose, which manifested in the form of countless whisky shots and beer chasers. I had been chatty and sociable—completely unlike myself.

There had been that cute blonde girl, the one whose smile reminded me of—wait—

I slowly turned my aching head around and saw a tangle of blonde hair poking out of the covers on the pillow next to me.

"Oh, shit," I breathed.

I don't know if that had been enough to wake her, or if she had been lying there waiting, but the tangle of hair turned until a face appeared, inches away from mine.

"Good morning, Martin," she said.

As she said my name I realized I couldn't remember hers. *Sarah? Samantha? Something with an 'S'?*

"Good morning," I replied.

She surprised me with a kiss, but I felt nothing in return. I tried not to recoil, but I wanted to leap out of the bed.

Her hand snaked up my thigh, and I realized I was completely naked. This time I did recoil, sitting up and turning away from her.

"Hey there, I —oh," I felt the room spin, and I dove back down into my pillow, holding on for dear life.

"You were pretty drunk last night," her voice hovered nearby.

"You don't say," I replied, trying not to sound sarcastic and failing miserably. I began to consider what would be more embarrassing: sprinting naked to the bathroom, or just barfing my brains out in bed.

I took several deep breaths and tried to focus on stopping my equilibrium from spinning the room. All I needed were a few moments of quiet to focus—

"I've seen you at work a few times," she droned on, "I'm glad you finally came up and talked to me. I've never dated a guy from work before."

The guilt she was heaping on wasn't making me feel any better. I'd never dated anyone from work before either, although I was pretty sure neither one of us believed the foggy events of the previous night qualified as a "date".

Dates outside of work were also uncommon, and nurturing any of them into an actual relationship felt like an anthropological mystery to me.

My continued silence seemed to get through, and I felt her move away to the far side of the bed. Out of curiosity, I snuck a peek out from under my pillow as she pulled on the T-shirt I had been wearing the night before. The extra weight she carried made her quite voluptuous, although a true lover's eye would have been much more forgiving of her natural flaws. When she bent over to pick up another discarded piece of clothing, I felt myself stiffen a little. I buried my face back into the pillow, cursing myself for making matters worse. Now I definitely couldn't make a run to the bathroom without looking like I was attempting the pole vault.

"Oh wow, you're an astrophysicist *and* an engineer? You didn't tell me that last night," she said. I looked out from my pillow again and saw her looking at the pair of degrees hanging on my wall. "Now I'm even more impressed."

"Uh… what exactly *did* I tell you last night?" I asked.

"You were telling me about the boarding school you got sent to. How you felt like you were sent into exile because it was out in the middle of nowhere," she said, moving to my bookshelf and looking at the stacks of textbooks.

"You actually studied all of these?"

"I did."

"What got you so interested in all this stuff in the first place?" she asked.

It's like a million little stars are falling from the sky!

The sudden tingling sensation of melting snowflakes on my tongue made me catch my breath as my pulse raced.

"A friend," I exhaled.

"Oh?" she said with a little too much interest.

I needed to deflect.

"The boarding school was out in the middle of nowhere," I said, "But it had an amazing view of the stars. That was when I really got hooked. Started visiting the library to pick up books about stars and space, and I haven't stopped since."

"Cool," she said, continuing her archaeological exploration of my room.

The world had stopped spinning enough for me to try lifting my head, but it still felt like my entire brain was throbbing.

I stole another look at the girl as she walked around in my T-shirt with her back to me. She certainly wasn't unattractive. I remembered having seen her around the office, but I didn't have clue which department she belonged to.

Mary? Maria? Maddy? Maybe her name starts with an 'M' instead…

Whatever her name was, she hadn't snuck out in the middle of the night. She seemed genuinely interested in me. So why did I already have my back up, hoping that she would just leave already? Why couldn't I for once just take a chance and see where this might go? Things may have started off on the wrong foot, but I hadn't scared her off yet. There was still a chance to turn this into something.

Even as the thought occurred to me, I felt a sort of paralysis take over, preventing me from moving or speaking. I didn't know what to do or say next, so I just froze and stared at her.

She must have felt my eyes on her, because she turned around to face me.

"Feeling any better?" she asked.

I shrugged and nodded.

She came over and sat down on the bed next to me. I had to fight my urge to move away. But this time I think she could sense my apprehension

"Do you want me to go?" she asked.

Yes.

"No," I said, "Of course not."

"You just seem… a little uncomfortable," she leaned in.

"Not at all," I replied, and met her lips with a kiss.

I wanted there to be a spark this time—I wanted it so badly, believing I could magically conjure up an emotional connection with that kiss.

But there was nothing.

This was just a play, and I was only an actor.

Samantha!

The name appeared in my head and it clicked with the face I was kissing. Unfortunately, it was the only thing clicking.

She broke away from the kiss and looked into my eyes. I could see the disappointment in her expression. The words from my lips had told her one thing, but the kiss had exposed them as a lie.

"This isn't going to go anywhere, is it?" she asked, not wanting an answer.

I scrambled for something to say. "Maybe we just need to start over, *Samantha*."

I thought perhaps hearing me say her name would stir something between us.

It did.

I saw her flinch, and her expression darkened.

"What did you call me?"

The name that had clicked with such certainty in my mind before began to slip and grind gears.

"Sam…?" I dug myself deeper.

She got up and started grabbing her clothes, pulling them on quickly.

"Jesus, you don't even know my name," she said, her voice shaking.

I thought I had felt horrible before, but it didn't compare to this.

"I'm sorry—I was very drunk last night," I started to ramble, "I'm probably still a little drunk. I'm sure once I completely sober up, I'll remember everything."

She didn't turn to look at me.

"Forget it," she said, and then let out a humorless laugh. "But I guess you already have now, haven't you?"

I didn't have a reply. I wished I knew the words to stop her from walking out the door, but I didn't.

So she left.

She left, still wearing my favorite T-shirt; a *John Carter of Mars* art print by Frank Frazetta.

There was no way I was going to ask for it back.

"Bye-bye Barsoom," I sighed.

CHAPTER 6

Mars orbit, 2025

At long last, the day arrives.

Seven months, fourteen days and two hours since leaving Earth, we have reached Mars.

Our excitement is tempered with a new anxiety. We've just made the furthest manned trip through space in history, but crossing the finish line is what will most likely kill us. Today we either make history, or we'll *be* history.

The first task is to get our engines back online and steer our speeding metal bullet into orbit so that we don't punch a new crater into the planet.

Despite being idle for months, our steering thrusters come back online, firing in perfect unison and flipping the capsule over. I feel more than a little anxious as Mars rolls out of sight from our cockpit window, our beacon of hope disappearing for the first time.

Once we've corrected our trajectory, a new short countdown for main engine ignition begins. I try not to think about the consequences if nothing happens when the countdown runs out. But when the time comes the main engine responds with a definitive roar. It will take a full thirty minutes of engine burn to slow us down enough for Mars' gravity to latch on to us.

It's not long before Mars makes its glorious return, its massive red face filling our cockpit window as we pass by, so incredibly close I can see the separation between the dusty atmosphere and the planet's surface.

Finally, the main engine cuts off into silence. I can feel the knot in my stomach tighten as I watch Mars continue to shrink away.

"Come on, come on," I mutter, "Grab on…!"

Moments later, the stars in our cockpit window begin to slide as Mars' invisible fingers pull our spacecraft back towards the planet.

Jomo checks his readings and I can hear his sigh of relief over the comm.

"Mars Alpha to mission control, we have achieved orbit," Jomo transmits, and then looks over at me. "Well my diaper is full, how about yours?"

We both laugh like giddy school kids until the knots in our stomachs loosen. Then there is a new sensation.

"Can you feel that?" I ask.

After months of hurtling weightless through space, my body can actually sense the pull of the planet below.

Jomo nods, "Amazing."

Because of the vast distance our radio signal has to travel, our cheering section won't get the news for another ten minutes, so it's up us to provide the celebration.

I hold up my fist. "Top shelf, brother."

"What is on the top shelf?" asks Jomo.

"No, no—it's an expression. It means we're supposed to bump fists."

"This is a popular expression?"

"Well, yeah."

"Then why after all these years together have you never used this before?"

It's hard to tell if he's genuinely perplexed, or if he's just trying to wind me up with his dry straight-man routine.

"Because it's only appropriate to use when you arrive in orbit over an alien planet," I reply, "Now shut up and top shelf me."

Without any change in expression, he lifts his fist to mimic mine.

"Close enough," I say, reaching over and completing the fist bump.

This is only a momentary reprieve: the most perilous part is coming up next.

While we wait for more instructions from Earth, we gaze down on our new red home rotating beneath us.

The sense of awe I remembered feeling before when I looked down on Earth returns, but with a whole new set of emotions. I am overwhelmed knowing that we are the first human eyes to witness this view. Mars has a breathtaking foreign beauty about it—a unique palette of colors mixed with the occasional frothy swirl of a dust storm.

The unfamiliar landscape is also unsettling. While both planets feel like living creatures, their personalities couldn't be any more different. The Earth reflected a peaceful serenity, while Mars radiates a subtle menace. However I can't pretend to be surprised; I knew from the beginning this was going to be an abusive relationship.

We orbit for several more hours as we confirm the programmed landing details in a tedious, staggered conversation with mission control. Once we're done, it's back down to business, and the stomach knots begin to tighten once again. Jomo and I both take our anti-nausea pills, anticipating the toll gravity will take on us upon its return.

"We're gonna end up puking in these things, aren't we?" I say as I'm about to lock my helmet on.

"Yes," Jomo replies. "Try to keep it off your face shield if you can—won't be much help if either of us can't see out of our helmets."

I search for a witty comeback, but my nerves have made me too tense.

"Fantastic…" is all I can mutter as I lock on my helmet and strap myself in.

"Martin," Jomo says. I look over at him.

"Whatever happens now, I'm glad I was able to be here to share it with you, my brother," he says, holding out his hand.

"Yeah Jomo," I exhale, "Me too."

His sentiment hits me hard. I try to reach over and take his hand, but the seat straps make it impossible. Our fingers grasp at air, inches apart. I nod to him instead, and then turn away to fight back the welling tears before they float over my eyes and blind me.

One last short burn nudges us towards the planet and our orbit quickly deteriorates as we plummet down into the Martian atmosphere. The growl of our capsule vibrating fills my ears and our pod shakes as if in the teeth of a hungry predator. Gravity's long-awaited return punches my stomach up into my throat as we freefall through the red sky. My veins suddenly feel like they're filled with lead as terminal velocity crushes me under my own weight.

And then a new, louder and more violent roar snarls to life as the landing thrusters kick in. Sudden deceleration sends spider webs of pain out through my spine and across my back, but I can feel some of the weight pressing down on me begin to lift.

I struggle to read the altimeter to see how far we have left, but everything around me is an impossible blur of vibration. Once again, all I can is hold my breath and hope it's not my last.

Everything slows down as I can feel us begin to pull back from our downward plummet. As I'm crushed into my seat with tremendous force, every last bit of air is squeezed out of my lungs. I hear Jomo gasp in pain over the comm.

The weight begins to lift as our descent slows. I feel like I might be able to take a breath—then the thrusters cut off, dropping us several feet until we hit the ground. The impact is like getting rear-ended at a stoplight; a violent shock, but not crippling. The pod quivers for a moment, and then comes to a complete stop as the propulsion system powers down.

HOLY SHIT—WE MADE IT!!

The silence is as deafening as our landing. Jomo and I look at each other in disbelief that we have both managed to survive it all unharmed. I try to catch my breath and clear my throat. Choked with emotion, my voice sounds unfamiliar to me as I broadcast over the radio.

"Touchdown confirmed. Repeat, Mars Alpha has landed, and we are both five by five."

It will be ten minutes before mission control knows that our landing was a success, and another ten minutes before we can hear them celebrating, but I already feel the rush of an entire planet cheering.

As soon as I click off the comm, Jomo lets out a ferocious scream. I'm startled for a moment until I realize it's a primal release of pure joy. I've never seen Jomo euphoric before, but it feels very contagious.

"WE DID IT!!" I shout at the top of my lungs.

"Yes, yes, YES!!" Jomo shouts back, "We made it! We are here!"

"And we're alive!" I add.

"Oh yeah!" Jomo holds up his fist, "Come on Martin—hit the top drawer."

I burst out laughing.

"What?" Jomo asks.

"Nothing, nothing. Close enough. You are top drawer, indeed."

I unbuckle my straps so I can reach over and give him a solid fist bump.

The next several hours are a return to torture as we go over more endless checklists. Everything must be confirmed before we get the green light to exit the capsule. The first challenge facing us is standing up. Even on a planet with one third of Earth's gravity it's still a struggle to move. My head feels so heavy to my weakened neck muscles that just keeping it raised is tiring. Also, after seven months without gravity, my inner ear does not enjoy being told which way is up. My stomach enjoys it even less. Once we confirm there's no hull breach and the air in the capsule is still breathable, Jomo and I race to rip off our helmets. It's a relief not to fight against the nausea anymore. It's an even greater relief that the pills we popped bought us enough time to use the barf bags. Since I was too nervous to eat earlier, the recycled fluids I drank to keep hydrated before re-entry are all I retch out. Once I come up for air, I look at the contents sloshing around in the bag.

"I really don't remember drinking this much fluid today," I gasp, trying to catch my breath.

"The best part is we still have to recycle it," Jomo says, "So we get to drink it again later."

"Ah, the circle of life."

During our training, we were warned it would take weeks for our bodies to readjust to gravity. On Earth, astronauts returning from extended spaceflights have a support team who carry them from the capsule to the extraction vehicles. Then they are transported to a medical facility to recuperate, supervised by a team of scientists and physicians. Jomo and I have none of that. We will begin our tenure on Mars weak and nauseated, with only each other for support. But despite this, the excitement of what lies outside is enough of a motivator for us to suck it up and move on.

Fortunately, preparations have already been made for our arrival. A team of construction rovers, sent to Mars before we started training, established a rudimentary base camp. One of the rovers was dispatched from base camp to come and pick us up. Our very own Martian welcome wagon.

Finally, we are given the green light to open the hatch.

After locking our helmets back on, I let Jomo do the honors. As he twists the handles that release the pressure seal, we hear a loud gasp as the Martian atmosphere sucks the air out in a single breath. Jomo swings the hatch open wide and struggles through the small opening in an awkward crouch. I help him out by giving his backside an extra two-handed push, while making sure his spacesuit doesn't catch on anything on the way out.

I hear Jomo shout over the radio.

"Hhhhooooo…!"

I can't wait. Fighting the enormous fatigue from my unadapted muscles, I grasp the edges of the hatch and crawl out through the opening.

In my impatience, I miss the handhold outside of the hatch and tumble forward into empty space. Falling the few feet to the ground is a sensory shock after months of being weightless, but the low impact landing is much more forgiving than it would have been back on Earth.

I lay still for a moment, cursing myself for being so clumsy and risking a suit puncture. But I don't hear any warnings alarms or feel any change in pressure or temperature anywhere on my body.

"You okay?" Jomo asks, offering me a gloved hand.

"Yeah," I reply. "That's one small trip for man, one giant tumble for mankind, right?"

Jomo laughs as he pulls me to my feet. My gaze focuses on the Martian landscape in front of me.

It's so beautiful.

My eyes have thirsted for this moment, and I feel lightheaded as they take in the first drink of the panorama. Its barren geography has only a few rocky outcroppings in any direction, and yet this absolute emptiness somehow gives it a majestic beauty. The scale and depth of the landscape all around us is awe-inspiring.

I look over into Jomo's helmet and I can tell by his open-mouthed expression that he feels the same emotions.

The cameras on our helmets are running and I remember that this moment will be transmitted and witnessed by billions of eyes, millions of miles away.

Now *this* is a Neil Armstrong moment.

Since Jomo always claims he's terrible at speaking in two different languages, it has been left to me to verbally mark the milestone. Fortunately, I've had months to prepare.

"Yesterday we walked on the Moon," I begin. "Today we

walk on Mars. Tomorrow, anything is possible."

CHAPTER 7

Earth, 2019

W hen I logged in and saw Gwen's friend request, I couldn't believe my eyes. Our last goodbye suddenly felt like it was only yesterday. Her memory was frozen as part of my childhood and stored away in a place I wished was easier to forget.

My hands shook as I clicked to confirm her request, then I immediately jumped to Gwen's page to cyber stalk. My hopes were dashed when I saw that she was married, and, almost as hard to believe, she was a mother. She had a six-year-old son named Sebastian.

It wasn't long after I accepted her friend request that Gwen followed up with her first message. She apologized for losing touch, and blamed herself for not doing more to track me down earlier. She was quite impressed with my career choice and sounded very proud of my accomplishments.

Our correspondence continued with surprising frequency over the next few months. I learned that Gwen had become an elementary school teacher in a town just outside of Toronto. She enjoyed her students and summers off, but couldn't help feeling a little disappointed she had given up on her own dream of going into space.

Over time, the tone of her writing became more open—almost flirtatious—but I convinced myself it was just wishful thinking. Although she was always happy to share stories about her son Sebastian, the subject of her husband never came up. It was a strange omission, and yet I hesitated to ask because I was afraid of the answer. So I played along, pretending he didn't exist, living in constant fear that some small slip on my part might scare her away.

Then one day I received the most surprising message yet: Gwen said she would be visiting Montreal during the summer and wanted to know if we could get together for coffee. We set the date for a few weeks' time, which meant a lot of sleepless nights during the wait. When I wasn't distracting myself, my mind would race with possible scenarios and imaginary conversations. Everything would always lead to that momentary lull in conversation, where we would look into each other's eyes, and then some invisible force would push us closer until I could feel her breath on my lips…

I would snap out of the daydream with my heart pounding. Just the thought of that kiss felt like a violation of our friendship. Guilt wouldn't let me imagine more, but my conscience was tempered by the fear of how devastating her rejection would be.

The day of our reunion finally arrived, and after yet another sleepless night and several wardrobe changes, I left for the coffee shop almost an hour early.

I walked in and looked around for the perfect spot to watch the door. I had already scanned the café twice before I noticed a woman looking at me. The look of surprise on her face caught my attention, but when I saw her eyes looking back at me, the abyss of time between us fell away.

Gwen.

She looked up and smiled, and once again I was that boy who had found the one girl in the entire universe he truly loved.

"Hi," Gwen said.

"Hi," was my witty comeback.

"You look—" she started.

"You too." I finished.

I sat down. Gwen reached across and touched my hand as if to check that I was real. I was surprised that her hands felt as sweaty as mine. I was mesmerized by her face, amazed now that I was seeing her in person how little she had changed.

She stared back at me, but soon her blue eyes brimmed with tears and her lips trembled.

"What's wrong?" I asked.

"I never got the chance to properly thank you for what you did that night," Gwen said.

"You don't need to…" I said.

"Yes, I do," she replied.

And with that, she leaned over and kissed me.

A jolt of electricity shot through my entire body. Before I could take hold of my senses I suddenly jumped back in shock.

She looked at me, trying to read my surprised expression.

"Martin?"

"That was…" I tried.

"Yeah," she agreed.

None of the scenarios that had played out in my mind had ever gone like this. I struggled to remember the basic courtesies of conversation.

"Do you want to order some coffee?" I asked.

"I actually don't like coffee," Gwen replied, "More of a tea person."

"Oh, okay. So… do you want some tea?"

"No."

"Oh," I said.

I didn't know what to say next. So we sat there, looking at each other. She held my hands lightly in her own, running her thumbs back and forth over my fingers, sending little shivers up and down my arms. She smiled and let out a nervous laugh. I couldn't help smiling back.

"I guess I should confess," I said, "I don't really drink coffee either."

Gwen's nervous laugh turned into a fit of giggles.

"Best. Coffee. Date. EVER."

"Date?"

"Sorry, should I have used another word?" Gwen asked.

"No, no. I like that word," I replied, "In fact, I love it."

"Love? Now you're the one using dangerous words," she said.

"Sorry…"

We both sank into silence again for a moment.

"So we're both using dangerous words, and we're both sorry," Gwen said, "Now what?"

"Good question. Now what?"

"Maybe we should stop talking," she said.

Even I could take a hint.

"You wanna get out of here?"

She nodded.

We left.

There wasn't much need for awkward conversation after that. The cab ride home was a beautiful blur of kissing and heavy petting. At one point I could see the cab driver watching us in his rearview mirror with an annoyed look in his eyes, but I was well past caring about anything beyond Gwen.

We stumbled through the door into my townhouse hallway like a drunken pair of dancers. Buttons popped, zippers were ignored, and by the time we reached the stairs we were both completely naked. Getting the rest of the way up the steps at that point seemed futile, so she mounted me there. The edge of the steps slammed into my spine, but the pleasure far outweighed the pain.

My climax arrived far sooner than I expected, sending an overdose of endorphins tingling through my brain. Gwen collapsed on me, sweaty but still electric. I crushed her into me, like a drowning man, unwilling to let go.

Once the sensation returned back into my limbs, I relaxed

my grip and dared to look at her. I brushed her hair back so I could see her face. There was that same wild mix of emotions there, but then she smiled.

"I hope that lived up to expectations," Gwen said.

"And then some." I exhaled.

"You have a bed in this place?" she asked.

"I hope so," I replied. "Otherwise I'm going to end up crippled with an ass full of splinters."

Gwen laughed as she released me and stood up. She pulled me up to my feet and the nerves along my spine stung in protest.

"Ow," I groaned.

"Come on old man, I'm not done with you yet…" Gwen said as she took my hand and led me to the bedroom.

I looked up at her and marveled at every dimple and curve of her flesh. I would follow that beautiful backside anywhere.

The afternoon spilled into the evening, and then into the early hours of the morning. There was very little conversation, just two bodies existing as one, shutting out the rest of the world. It felt like neither one of us wanted to spoil the moment by saying anything that might bring reality crashing down on us.

Every muscle ached and I felt like I was spent to the last molecule of my being, but I had never felt so happy. If heaven existed, it wasn't some boring toga party with harps and wings up in the clouds, it was *this*. I wanted this moment of cosmic perfection to last forever.

I stared at Gwen's head as it rested on my chest, and wondered what she was looking at. I followed her gaze and saw the clock.

"Your son isn't waiting up for you I hope," I said, finally breaking the silence.

"He's with his dad for the weekend," Gwen replied.

"Oh, good…"

We lapsed into silence again. But for some reason, now that the subject had been broached, the quiet bothered me. There would never be a good time to ask the question, but after how we had spent the last several hours, I needed an answer.

"I know I'm going to regret asking this, but—"

"You don't need to ask," Gwen cut in. "We've been… on a break for some time now."

"Oh," I said.

"I know that still doesn't make this right. Do you hate me now?" Gwen asked.

"No. I'd gladly burn in all seven levels of hell for this," I joked, running my fingers over her bare flesh, the source of my damnation.

Gwen turned to look at me and I was surprised to see that sadness again in her eyes. My poor attempt at humor had opened some old wound, and now I'd see what spilled out.

"I need to explain," she said.

"You don't."

"Please," she said, so heartbroken that I couldn't refuse her.

I nodded for her to continue.

"I got pregnant with Sebastian when Tom and I had just started dating," Gwen began. "He did what he thought was the honorable thing by marrying me. But even before Sebastian was born, Tom and I both knew that we weren't right for each other."

It was the first time she had ever mentioned her husband's name. Such a simple name for the imposing figure I had created out of my own insecurity.

"Trying to raise a kid together only made things worse between us," Gwen continued. "Showing up late each night after work turned into nights where he just didn't show up at all. Then one night he came home, but he was drunk and had a chip on his shoulder. He was shouting, and then I was shouting… I was so angry, but also scared. I told him to get out, and eventually he left, but I was shaking… It brought back all of those memories of my dad… I always swore to myself I wouldn't put up with that again. I certainly didn't want that sort of life for Sebastian."

"You did what you had to do," I said.

"In his heart, Tom is a good guy and a good father to Sebastian. He never got violent, and I hope he never will, but I wasn't going to take that chance. We're better friends now that we're apart. Sometimes I think two people work better when they're not living under the same roof. We should get a divorce, make it official, but it's pretty expensive and things have been confusing enough for Sebastian."

"Makes sense," I said. "I hope I haven't made things even more confusing."

This time I was relieved to see Gwen smiling at me.

"No, you haven't. If anything, you've made things clearer. I've been so busy trying to do what I thought was the right thing, I didn't trust that following my heart for once could be it."

"So this," I waved a finger between us. "This is you following your heart?"

Gwen crawled up my chest until I could feel the breath from her lips on mine.

"Yes."

"I like the sound of that," I said.

"Me too," she replied and kissed me.

When we came up for air, I suddenly felt overwhelmed as the reality of my childhood dream coming true began to sink in.

"I never believed this moment would ever happen," I said, my eyes tearing up. "I never thought you would ever feel the same way that I felt about you."

She looked surprised. "You mean you didn't know?"

"Know what?"

"That I fell in love with you from the first moment we met," Gwen replied. "I fell in love with the little boy and his telescope—the little boy who fell so hard for me he had the wind knocked out of him."

The revelation felt overwhelming and yet a little sad.

"No, I didn't know. It might have made the past few decades a little easier on me. You never said anything."

"We were both kids. What did we know about being in

love? I think that by not saying anything, we didn't get a chance to ruin it."

"And now?" I asked.

"I think we're long overdue for making some new mistakes," she said.

And with that, Gwen kissed me again. But this time it felt different. It felt like a kiss with a million possibilities and a promise for a future I had only dreamed of.

Her hand crept downwards, and despite our previous marathon session I was ready again. I rolled over and kissed her—not just as a lover, but as her true love.

I couldn't help thinking how it all just felt so…

So *perfect*.

CHAPTER 8

Mars, 2026

The view outside my door is like no other, and I am one of two people in the entire universe privileged enough to witness it. It's amazing how different things look from the surface compared to orbit. For one thing, the landscape isn't very red at all. The frozen Martian soil is a greenish brown color, and most rock formations look blue-grey with only a few patches of red sand in between. Depending on how much dust is blowing on a given day, the sky overhead ranges in palette from grey-green, to light tan, all the way to burnt orange. We are in a flat area with very few rocky outcroppings—or anything else for that matter. The view is a panorama in most directions. On a clear day you can see forever, with the landscape curving away into the horizon.

Twice a day, the misshapen moon Phobos rises in the west, only a third the size of Earth's. A second moon called Deimos is no more visible than a bright star as it orbits in the opposite direction. The days themselves are slightly longer than Earth's, and yet each year is almost twice as long. It's very easy to move around, even with a bulky spacesuit. Although after seven months of being weightless and nearly a year spent on Mars, it's hard to remember exactly how much heavier I felt back on Earth. Walking on Mars is not quite as serene as floating in space, but there is still a dance-like elegance to it. And while my standing leaps on Mars are not nearly as impressive as those accomplished by Burrough's John Carter, they would still shatter the distance record of any Olympian back on Earth.

My view of the stars at night trumps it all. On a clear night, the thin atmosphere gives me an unobscured panorama of the galaxy just beyond my doorstep. The stars hang like tiny jewels in the blackness, just out of reach. Even our long voyage among the stars cannot compare. Viewing the stars through a small cockpit window feels insignificant when you can look up and see the entire universe unfurled above your head.

I still view the stars from the other side of a face shield on my spacesuit's helmet, but since I'd be dead in seconds if I took it off, I'm pretty much okay with that.

Jomo and I have settled comfortably into the small base camp habitat, and even managed a minor expansion, using our old capsule. When we first arrived, we were both a little nervous about just how ready the base camp would be to support its new residents, given that the initial construction was relayed over millions of kilometers to a small team of robots. We were relieved to discover everything online and operational, especially since we were so exhausted and nauseated we just wanted to curl up and sleep for a week.

But unlike returning to Earth after a prolonged spaceflight, it didn't take months for us to recover. Mars' reduced gravity allowed us to be back up and productive by the end of our first week. And with the initial base camp comprised of only three attached landers, we were eager to expand our new home.

Once we both felt able to handle the trip, Jomo and I took a pair of transport rovers back across the Martian landscape to retrieve our lander. With the rovers' slow and dependable tank treads, it took several hours to reach our landing coordinates, but we were too busy enjoying the view to notice.

Although nothing looked familiar along the way, the coordinates guided us straight back to our parking spot. It was an odd mix of nostalgia and revulsion seeing the capsule again. I felt like an escaped convict re-visiting my prison cell.

"I can't believe how small it looks now," Jomo said over the radio.

"I hear ya," I replied.

Neither one of us had any interest in going back inside, so we focused on hooking up the capsule to both rovers for the extra slow trip back, with our bounty in tow.

It took us several days to reconfigure base camp and attach our capsule. But once attached, we were able to add on to it with inflatable compartments, eventually increasing our habitable indoor living space twenty fold. The material was similar to our spacesuits, with interwoven Kevlar fibers and multiple layer redundancies to guard against punctures and leaks. But needless to say, anything with sharp edges was always handled with a measured sense of caution.

To better power our expanded base camp, we unrolled a series of flexible solar panels to capture the intense solar radiation permeating the thin atmosphere. While the new panels do a great job powering all our equipment, the reserve batteries only last five days running minimum life support. Unlike the solar arrays we used to power our capsule across space, on the planet's surface there's always a fine veil of dust blowing around, so keeping the solar panels clean requires our daily attention. Some dust storms on Mars have been known to last several months. If such a storm were to settle in over our base camp, the next team to arrive would likely find a tomb.

While the amount of solar radiation passing though Mars' thin atmosphere is great for powering base camp, it isn't so great for the human body. To create a better protective barrier we had to cover the habitat with Martian soil. This was a monumental task, especially since the soil was so densely packed. While the rovers have some digging capability, they're more like a kid in a sandbox with a toy shovel. Any decent construction digger back on Earth would finish the job in a few hours. But we had to make do with the equipment on hand.

Besides protection from radiation, the other wonderful thing the soil provides is water. Although dry and dusty on the surface, just a few feet below, the soil is more like mud. Our base camp location was chosen for the concentration of water found in the soil on earlier rover explorations. Once this Martian mud is brought back to the habitat, it's processed through our equipment to extract the water. After a full load, each extraction gives us enough water to drink for a day, with enough left over to wet a cloth and have an astronaut's version of a luxurious bath. One thing is for sure—it definitely beats our previous rations of recycled pee.

The water can also be further broken down into its base oxygen molecules. Combined through special filters with the nitrogen and argon gasses already in the Martian atmosphere, we are able to breathe air that is quite similar to that on Earth while inside the habitat.

With water also comes the ability to grow our own produce using hydroponics and fertilized by human waste broken down with microorganisms. For someone who never gardened, I've become quite adept at growing my own food. While sheer survival is always a helpful motivator, after almost a year of pre-packaged rations, the thought of having freshly grown food has turned gardening into my favorite obsession.

The most curious thing about living on Mars has been the reaction back on Earth. Apparently Jomo and I have become major celebrities on the big blue marble. The video feeds we've set up, along with our video journals, are edited together into a weekly reality show documenting our progress.

"The Red Colony" is a ratings hit, and not only helps repay our investors, but secures funding for more resources in the future. While I may never sign any autographs, the audience for "Martin the Martian's" social media feed grows exponentially every day. It's a strange dichotomy to be so physically alone while still being virtually connected to millions, who hang on every word and photo I post back across the galaxy.

It's very gratifying knowing that what you do has such a profound impact on others. The messages from complete strangers telling us how much Jomo and I inspire them gives me strength on my darker days. Keeping it all together is a daily battle in an extreme situation such as this. Most of the mental battle is fought by keeping ourselves busy as much as possible, and leaving little time to dwell on the past or what we have left behind.

But even despite my best efforts, there are times I can't stop my mind from wandering off across the galaxy, back to the planet I once called home.

Even across this vast distance, I am still not free of Gwen. I have run as far away as possible, and yet I am still tethered to the memory of her. As much as I miss the Earth, I miss Gwen even more, because she was the one who made it feel like home.

I don't want to admit to myself that I still love her, though I already know it's the truth. But I've gone too far and can't turn back.

Even so, I still can't help but wonder if it would have all been easier if we had just had the chance to say goodbye.

CHAPTER 9

Earth, 2019

S ebastian, this is my friend Martin," Gwen said.
His eyes darted up to look at me for a moment, and then returned to their previous fixed spot on the ground.

"Hi," he mumbled.

I knelt down and held out my hand.

"Hi Sebastian, it's great to meet you. Your mom talks about you all the time," I said, "She says you're pretty cool."

His eyes, set in dark circles on his pale face, didn't move from the floor. He was a skinny, quiet kid that looked like the next gust of wind might take him away.

"Sebi, he wants to shake your hand," Gwen said.

"You're not supposed to shake hands," Sebastian said, craning his head around to look at his mother, leaning into her and away from me.

"What do you mean?" Gwen asked.

"My teacher said you get germs that way," Sebastian explained.

"Lovely," Gwen shook her head, "Did she also tell you it's rude not to?"

He sighed in defeat, and then turned back to me, stretching out a fist.

"Props?" I asked, also closing my hand into a fist.

"No. you're supposed to say 'top shelf'," he replied.

"Right—top shelf!" I said, holding out my fist.

He bumped his bony knuckles against mine. I made an explosion noise and fluttered my fingers as our fists parted. His eyes finally lifted to look at me, but he didn't look amused.

"What," I said, "aren't you supposed to make an explosion sound after?"

"No."

Despite his answer, I saw a brief smirk twist the corner of his mouth.

It was a start.

"Looks like people are going in," Gwen said, looking over her shoulder, "You ready, Sebi?"

"What's this movie called again?" Sebastian asked.

"I told you already, this isn't a movie theater, it's a planetarium." Gwen said.

"What's a planet aquarium?" Sebastian asked.

Gwen laughed. "No—a *planetarium.*"

Sebastian still looked confused.

"It's like a spaceship that lets you explore the stars without having to leave Earth," I explained.

I could see my explanation sinking in through the veil of shyness, until he finally nodded.

"Cool," he said.

I looked up at Gwen and saw the same surprised look of hope.

Progress.

Gwen and I had agreed to take things slow with Sebastian, keeping up the image of two childhood friends who just wanted to catch up on old times. Sebastian was still both physically and emotionally fragile. He was just a kid trying to comprehend the growing abyss between his parents.

"You know Sebi, Martin's job is to study space and the

stars," Gwen said as we funneled our way through the doors and into the theater.

"Are you an astronaut?" Sebastian asked.

"Not yet, but maybe one day," I replied.

"Astronauts are cool," he said.

"See, now you have to become one," joked Gwen.

We settled into our seats, Gwen strategically putting Sebastian between us. He slumped down, seeming exhausted at the effort.

"Late night?" I asked Gwen.

"He gets tired easily," she said, "I think he might have asthma, the way sometimes he loses his breath. I made an appointment to see a specialist when we get back home."

"Now I feel guilty for wanting the summer to last forever," I said, "It's already flying by way too quickly."

"Try being a parent," Gwen replied, "It's the worst time machine ever. It only goes forward, and the button is always stuck on fast forward. It's felt like that since the day Sebi was born."

"Yeah, being a kid felt like forever to me," I said, "In some ways, I'm still that kid."

"Yes you are," Gwen winked at me.

The theater darkened and the first images of the cosmos were projected on the dome above us. I snuck a glance at Sebastian as he stared upwards. His mouth had dropped open in awe.

"I think he likes it," Gwen whispered.

"Just like some other kid I once knew," I whispered back.

Gwen smiled and settled back into her reclined seat, as the digital universe danced before our eyes.

CHAPTER 10

Mars, 2026

When you're only one of two people on a planet, it's hard not to notice that something's wrong.

Jomo has become more withdrawn the last few weeks, and I can tell he hasn't been sleeping very much. Whenever I ask him about it, he just laughs it off and tells me it's nothing. He claims he's just in a rut and trying to keep himself busy to help work through it. But there's something behind his forced smile that worries me. I know Jomo too well not to recognize when he's struggling with something serious. But I also know that I won't be able to make him share it with me before he's ready.

Then one night I awake with a start, my heart pounding in my ears. I try to think back, trying to remember the dream that woke me, but then I realize it wasn't that.

My unconscious memory tells me I heard a scream.

I leave my pod and go over to check on Jomo. He's curled up on the floor next to his cot, weeping.

I kneel down and touch his shoulder.

"Jomo, what is it?"

He recoils as I touch him and looks at me in fear, as though he expected to see someone else.

"Jomo, whatever this is you're going through," I say, "you have to tell me before it tears you apart."

He nods, but still has to take a moment to breathe and try to calm himself.

Finally, he's able to spit out two words:

"They're here."

The way he says it makes the hairs stand up on the back of my neck.

"Who? Who's here?"

"My wife. And my children. They are here. They have followed me here."

Now I understand why he never wanted to talk about it.

"Hey buddy, it's okay," I reassure him, even though I'm feeling far from reassured myself. "I'm no Dr. Lars, but you do know how crazy that sounds, right?"

Jomo just continues to stare ahead. "When I left behind my life in Kenya, I no longer dreamt of them. Not once. Not during our training. Not during our trip. But the first night here, I dreamt that I looked outside and saw my wife Jata holding our daughters in her arms. She looked up at me, but she had no eyes. Then my daughters turned to ash in her arms. She tried to scream, but then she too turned to ash."

"It's just dreams man," I say, scrambling to psychoanalyze, but feeling in over my head, "It's just your subconscious trying to work through some heavy stuff."

"It's more than just dreams," Jomo continues, "Now I also see them when I'm awake."

This revelation confirms that I'm out of my depth. "You mean, like hallucinations?"

"You can call them hallucinations," Jomo replies, "But to me, they are ghosts."

"How often do you see these hallucinations?"

"I see them all the time."

"All the time? Like just now? That's why you screamed?"

Jomo nods.

"But they're gone now, right?" I ask.

Jomo doesn't answer, but instead keeps staring straight ahead. A chill runs up my spine as I realize what he has been staring at all this time.

I force myself to turn around and look, with my heart pounding again in my ears. I am relieved to see the corner of the pod he's staring at is empty. But when I turn back, I can see from his expression that it's not empty for him.

"Who's there?" I ask Jomo, still not able to shake the chill tingling over me.

"Safika, my youngest," he says, not taking his tear-stained eyes off the spot, "She is in her white coffin, and it is filled with dirt. She is suffocating, trying to scream, trying to get herself out. She is looking at me, begging me to help her, but when I reach for her, she is not there. I cannot touch her—I am only allowed to watch her suffer."

"I'm sorry Jomo, but she isn't real. This is just your guilt talking. That and a lack of sleep has your mind playing tricks on you. It doesn't even make sense. She died in a fire. She wasn't buried alive."

"They are trying to tell me something," he says, "but I do not know what it is!"

My mind spinning, I grasp for an answer.

"I think they're telling you that no matter how far you run, you can't get away from yourself."

Finally, Jomo breaks his stare and turns to look at me.

"What do you mean?"

I'm wondering the same thing myself, so I try to follow the bread crumbs of my logic.

"You said you left your old life behind, but how is that possible if you never said goodbye?"

"I said goodbye at their funeral."

"You said goodbye to your wife and daughters, but then you ran away from the life you had with them. You never said goodbye to the part of you that you shared with them. You never said goodbye to the husband or to the father that you once were. When was the last time you spoke to your wife's family—or even your own?"

"At the funeral," Jomo says.

"Did they know you were planning to leave?"

Jomo shakes his head.

"Don't you think they would like to hear from you? The whole world knows about you, but they know who you really are. You are still their family."

Jomo turns his attention back to the corner of the pod and I see him jump and then look around.

"She's gone," he says with a hint of disappointment in his voice.

"Whether they're really ghosts or just hallucinations, I really think they'll leave you alone if you try reaching out to your family back on Earth."

Jomo agrees to test out my theory the following day. For that night though, what he needs most is sleep. I tell him I'll sit up and watch over him as he sleeps, to either help ward off spirits, or at least give him some measure of comfort that he's not alone.

It's an exhausting night, but I'm happy to see Jomo finally get some rest. Aside from a few twitches, he sleeps like a rock.

As I sit there I feel like I've relieved at least some small measure of Jomo's burden. Although I knew even as I said the words that my advice was filled with hypocrisy. Here I am, pushing Jomo to do the very thing I refused to do for myself. I am running from my past as much as he is.

And every time I look back, the view is terrifying.

CHAPTER 11

Earth, 2019

My phone rang and I smiled when I saw the picture of Gwen's smiling face appear on the display.

"Hey babe, how are you?"

But Gwen's voice sounded strained when she finally spoke. "Martin…"

"Gwen what's wrong?"

"Sebastian…"

My pulse began to race.

"What did the specialist say?"

"It's his heart."

Her voice was thick with anguish. I tried to speak but suddenly felt light-headed.

The truth behind his frail appearance now seemed so obvious; I felt stupid for not seeing it.

"I'll leave now and catch the next train," I said once I found my voice.

"No, don't," Gwen said. "Tom is here with us in the hospital. With everything going on, it will just make things more confusing for Sebastian having you here."

"I understand," I said, even though I couldn't bear being hundreds of miles away from her when I knew she needed me. "But if you change your mind I can be there right away."

"Thank you," Gwen said.

"Gwen, he's going to be okay," I said, "You have to say it. You have to believe it."

"I wish I did," Gwen replied with a strained whisper and hung up.

At the time I hoped it was merely a mother's worrying nature, but in the end she was right. Sebastian had a congenital heart defect and needed a transplant. They placed him on the donor list, but soon after his condition spiraled downward.

As the end grew near, Gwen grew distant. First our phone conversations were brief and distracted, and then she stopped returning my calls. After a week of being in limbo, I got desperate and tracked down another number to call.

"Hello?" the voice on the other end answered.

"Is this Marco?" I asked.

"Who's this?"

"My name is Martin. I don't know if you remember me, but we kind of knew each other as kids. I'm a... friend of your sister."

"Yeah, I know who you are."

I couldn't tell whether or not that was a good thing. Either way, I was desperate for information.

"The thing is, I've been trying to get some news about your nephew's condition, but I haven't heard anything from Gwen in a week."

"Oh," was all he said, leaving me hanging in a long, drawn-out silence.

"Hello?"

"He... He passed away."

The news was a knife to my chest. I couldn't believe such a beautiful little life had been snuffed out. I had dealt with a lot of loss in my life, but I couldn't imagine the magnitude of what Gwen was going through. The thought of her suffering made my heart ache even more.

"I'm… I'm so sorry," I replied in a daze. "When did it… When did he…?"

"Monday night. The viewing is on Friday. The funeral is Saturday."

There wasn't much else to say. I thanked him for the information and hung up.

I wrestled with going to the viewing and funeral, having not been invited or even informed, but in the end I went anyway. The old fear of everything slipping away was gnawing in my gut again, and something told me I had to confront my fear or be consumed by it.

When I arrived at the funeral home for the visitation, the place was packed, with people spilling out into the hallways, all of them there for Gwen's little boy. But the crowd of people wasn't the only thing making it difficult for me to go in. One glimpse of the little casket at the front of the room and out of nowhere, I felt dizzy and found myself gasping for air.

After a lifetime of being locked away in my subconscious, the childhood memory of my own brother's casket came flooding back to me in a panic attack.

I remembered the utter devastation, the first awakening to my own mortality, that feeling of being broken into a thousand shards of glass.

Looking at that tiny coffin I felt small too; once again the world was a big and scary place that didn't make any sense. When I was a boy, it was in moments like these that I would run into my mother's arms for comfort. Knowing that she too was long gone made me feel even more alone.

I closed my eyes, trying not to think about the curious stares from the other mourners around me, and focused on breathing. Then I concentrated on the sound of my heart hammering in my ears. I kept taking deep breaths until the pounding quieted.

I reminded myself that it was Gwen who had saved me back then, my angel out of the darkness, pulling me back up onto my feet. Now it was Gwen who had been left shattered, and I owed it to her to reach in and help her pick up the pieces.

Still shaking, I forced my legs to move forward into the room. I tried to look anywhere other than the casket to keep the panic from clawing its way out and overwhelming me again.

I spotted Marco standing at the end of the front row. He had grown into his father's looks, although more clean cut, in a suit a few sizes too small with a closely-cropped hairstyle that wasn't helping his head look any less square. Gwen told me he had become a financial advisor for a private firm, where he bullied people into buying mutual funds with steep back-end penalties.

For a moment, I wondered if Freddy-Bedwetty was also somewhere nearby. I had never thought to ask Gwen if her brother's acne-covered accomplice was still a buddy. I took a quick look around the room, but either he wasn't there, or he had grown up to look like an actual human being.

Sitting next to Marco was their mother. She appeared tiny and frail, sunken into her chair like all the air had run out of her. Gwen told me their mother had taken their father back a decade earlier after he developed liver complications and became seriously ill. Despite Gwen's objections she had stayed with him as his health continued to fail. Her mother claimed with the alcohol gone, the monster's mask had been lifted and he was once again the man she had loved. Whatever the circumstances, it didn't last long; he died from liver failure less than a year after she took him back.

Directly opposite the casket I saw the trembling silhouette of Gwen standing in a black dress. I couldn't see her face, but I could read the overwhelming pain from her body language, and my heart was crushed at the sight.

Unable to take it anymore, I cut in front of the condolences line and made my way to the family. A few brief handshakes later I stepped into Gwen's view. Her eyes were red and sunken, and the grief etched on her face had aged her. At first she just stared past me, like I wasn't there. But when I didn't move on down the line like the others, her eyes lifted to look at me, and I saw a moment of confusion cross her face. I opened my mouth to say something but no words came out.

Her eyes welled up with tears and her trembling became worse. As I stepped forward expecting her to reach out to me, instead Gwen recoiled and collapsed sideways onto the shoulder of the man standing next to her. I had never seen a picture of him, but my gut knew right away that it was her husband Tom. One look and the villain in my imagination fled, leaving nothing but the raw image of a grieving father. He looked as if he had poured out every last drop of emotion and had been left hollow. Without even looking at me he stretched out his hand with mechanical instinct to accept my condolences. I took his hand and shook it, mumbling, "I'm very sorry".

My heart had already broken before I finished saying the words.

Tom nodded and continued to look past me as though I only existed on some other plane of reality, far away.

I looked back at Gwen but she had her face buried in Tom's shoulder, trying to stifle her sobs. Tom rubbed her back and tried to whisper some words of strength into her ear.

I saw it now. I saw why Gwen had grown so distant. It wasn't just because of losing her son. In the midst of intolerable tragedy she had sought comfort on familiar ground, and now I was once again a stranger looking in from the outside. I was no longer a part of her world.

I skipped the rest of the condolences line and walked straight out of the funeral home. I caught a cab and headed back to the train station. I decided not to stay for the funeral after all.

The closer I got to home, the more I felt I wanted to just keep going. I wanted to run, I wanted to scream, I wanted to pound my fists into something that could shatter every bone and shred my flesh. The darkness that had followed me around my entire life opened up beneath me and swallowed me whole. I was falling, blind with rage at the cruelty of the world. I blamed the whole planet for being nothing but a curse to me my whole life.

I hated it.

I wanted to leave it behind, along with every bad memory it held.

By the time my train arrived back in Montreal, I had made up my mind.

I knew what I had to do.

CHAPTER 12

Mars, 2027

Our Martian colony is growing.

After two years of relative isolation, four new astronauts have arrived, increasing our total number of permanent residents to six.

This international group of pioneers now includes William, a geologist from England; Jesper, a chemical engineer from Denmark; Akane, a botanist from Japan; and Lina, a biologist from Russia.

The original plan for Alpha Team was also supposed to include four astronauts, but in the final year of planning that number shrank to just two. At the time it was explained to us that more gear was necessary for the establishment of the colony, and fewer astronauts meant less of a strain on the limited resources during the critical first stage. It sounded like a valid explanation at the time, although during our long journey, Jomo and I came up with a different theory. If our mission came to a fatal end, the human tragedy would have been limited to only two lives, and the risk of sending more astronauts for another attempt would have been more palatable for both investors and public opinion. Of course, it was just a theory.

However, with the success of Alpha One's mission, the travel bookings are quickly filling up. The next three mission teams have already been selected, with each launch window separated by the twenty-six months it takes for the two planets to reach their minimum orbiting distance.

For now though, the six of us together in Base Camp already feels like a population explosion. The living quarters were cramped at first, as they were unable to do much upon arrival except struggle with readjusting to gravity. But it was a welcome inconvenience in exchange for some new but familiar faces.

We already knew each other well from our years of training together in the program, so our reunion is an even more exciting cause for celebration.

"A toast," William says as we sit squeezed into the cantina for our first meal together, "To Martin and Jomo, the first humans to walk the surface of Mars. Though we may walk in your footsteps, we can never fill your shoes."

The others cheer our names in agreement, and not since I fell out of the lander on my first day have I felt quite so abashed.

"Very poetic of you William. Thank you," I say.

"Well, I had seven months to think something up," William laughs, "Besides, with my ugly mug, saying something clever is the only way I'll ever make an appearance on the show, next to you rock stars." He nods his head to the cameras recording our every move.

"I'm sure people must be sick of watching only the two of us by now," I say.

"Do you watch the show?" asks Akane.

"No," Jomo bluntly replies.

"We did, at the beginning," I add, "But after a while, watching yourself gets a little boring."

"Those of us who have been watching think you are anything but boring," says Lina.

I catch Jomo's look out of the corner of my eye. During those difficult few months, instead of editing it out, they instead chose to exploit Jomo's crumbling mental state. They said it added drama to the show.

Disconnecting all of the cameras for a week helped them realize the error in their judgment.

From that point on, Jomo was able to privately focus on getting better by reaching out to his remaining family on Earth. He says that taking my advice has helped him. While some nights are still plagued by nightmares, he says at least while he's awake, he's no longer haunted by the ghosts of his past.

"That's okay," Jomo replies, "I prefer to be boring."

"Not me," Jesper chimes in, "I've spent seven months being boring, it's time for a little excitement—starting with this party!"

William claps Jesper on the back. "Well, we might all be a bunch of science geeks, but for once we'll be able to say that we threw the best party on the planet!"

William and Jesper roar with laughter. The sound of it is infectious, and soon we all join in.

In that moment it feels pretty damn good to once again be surrounded by friends.

Once the weakness and nausea began to wear off, our new roommates are very eager to get to work, setting up additional gear and expanding the habitat. I remember the same feeling when I first arrived. Nothing like being cooped up in a tiny capsule for seven months to motivate you into getting things done.

Since then it's been like four bolts of energy buzzing around the habitat every waking moment. At first the commotion was a welcome change compared to all those years of isolation. But after a few weeks the buzz went from exciting to annoying. Two years is a long time to settle into a rhythm, and now I feel irked and out of synch. They are the house guests who will never leave because they can't. I look forward to everyone having their own expansion pod built and the enthusiasm wearing off.

Every so often I catch Jomo looking at them with the same weariness I've seen in my own reflection.

"When are they going home again?" Jomo asks me, rolling his eyes.

"Never," I reply.

"At least having the ladies here makes for more pleasant company," Jomo says.

I'm surprised. "Really?" I ask, "And which one do you think is more pleasant? Akane or Lina?"

Jomo chuckles, "Not like that my friend. I was a man who spent the happiest years of his life surrounded by four strong women. That is why I like having them here."

"Still—if it *was* like that—there are only four men and two women on this entire planet. Your chances could be pretty good."

"For someone who has experienced so many things in his life, there is still so little you see," Jomo says.

"What do you mean?"

"Come with me little brother."

I follow Jomo to the cantina where Akane and Lina are chatting with each other. Jomo stops me before we step into their line of sight.

"What?" I ask.

"Just watch," Jomo says.

Still confused, I turn and watch their conversation. I can't make out what they are talking about, but whatever Lina is saying, Akane appears to be very interested. She nods and laughs at every little thing Lina says. It looks like the bond they formed during their training and trip across space has made them very close friends. As I watch them I wonder if this is how Jomo and I look when we are alone talking to each other.

As Lina talks, one of her long black bangs snakes loose from behind her ear and tumbles across her forehead. Right away, Akane reaches over and sweeps the lock of hair back over Lina's ear. Their animated conversation doesn't even miss a beat.

"Oh," I say.

Jomo just nods.

The first romance on Mars has already begun to blossom—just not how I had expected. At least two hearts on this planet wouldn't be lonely anymore.

William and Jesper announce their own imminent arrival at the cantina with a loud conversation and William's boisterous laugh. The new crew meets up and the noise level skyrockets.

The weary look returns to Jomo's face as he walks back towards his pod. Feeling much the same, I also head away from all the noise.

When I need to rediscover my Zen, I cram myself into a corner of the pod with my headset and tablet and try to lose myself in the web. Our elliptical orbit is between 34 million and 250 million miles away from Earth at any one time, which means the communication lag time has a substantial variance and complete net access is impossible. But we are still able to download specific websites. At times it almost feels like I'm surfing in real time. I usually stick to the social networking platforms, sending photos and videos out to the hundreds of millions of fans hungry for every new thing I throw their way. I suppose my ego takes more than a little pleasure in being able to dazzle an entire planet with my daily life. Definitely one of the real perks of the job.

There are always so many questions sent to me, and I always try to answer as many I can. But there is one repeated question I have avoided answering:

"What do you miss most about Earth?"

It's a question I can't answer because I can only think of one thing, and it's the one thing I cannot say:

Gwen.

I thought running away would rid me of my obsession, but it didn't. I thought making it impossible for us to ever be together would help get me over her but is hasn't. My body has travelled millions of miles into space, yet my heart continues to orbit around the same sun. I can no longer deny the gravitational pull she has on me.

This is the fundamental truth I always return to, so why try to fight against the pattern of my own existence? Some things are so deeply ingrained in your molecular structure they can never be changed.

I remember the day I took my first steps towards becoming an astrophysicist. It wasn't under some starry night sky, but inside a library. I read a book that explained how human beings are made up of stars.

The universe began with hydrogen and helium, and when the hydrogen became exhausted, a star would explode in a supernova. This created new elements which dispersed across the universe, eventually forming the Earth and its inhabitants.

So when I look up into the night sky and feel the stars talking to me—feel that connection—I believe there is something deep within my atoms answering that call of kinship. There would be no life without the stars. And one day our own star will go supernova and create new and unimaginable things. It is inevitable that some day we will all return to stardust.

As I relive that sense of awe I felt when taking in this humbling revelation, I feel like I am finally able to move forward.

"What do I miss most about the Earth?" I write, "It is not something, but rather someone. That special someone that only comes around once in a lifetime. She is also the one that got away. But for that, I have only myself to blame. I thought I had her, but then I lost her. And instead of trying to get her back, I ran away. It is something which I will regret until my last breath. There is nothing I miss about the Earth, except for her. To her, I can only say that my love for you is ever present and everlasting, and will continue until both of us are nothing more than stardust."

When I log in the next day, my lovelorn post has gone viral. The share rate is at least ten times anything I've ever posted before, responses are through the roof, and several major news sites have picked it up. It seems like everyone is a sucker for the guy with a broken heart living on the planet next door. I also now have marriage proposals from hundreds of women—and more than a few men.

The disturbing effect of my confession is the pressure to identify my mystery woman. I'm forced to dodge, pointing out that I didn't name her because I wanted her to keep her privacy. But the public appetite, whet for human drama, isn't sated by my evasions. Now what I thought was my first step towards closure has instead become a misstep. I fear Gwen will be discovered and shoved into the spotlight, and then made to re-live the pain and suffering of our past because of me. I'm millions of miles from Earth, and yet I feel like that little kid in the park again, terrified of the bullies. But it's Gwen I'm terrified for, not myself. I can't stand the thought of hurting her again. I can only hope she is somewhere unreachable—somewhere removed from the pain of her former life.

And then one day out of the blue, I log in and there is a message from Gwen waiting for me.

It reads: "I can't write the way that you can, so I sent a video instead. Please watch. Thanks, Gwen."

I realize that I've stopped breathing. I hesitate as I look at the attached video. Once again I am standing in front of a doorway I didn't think I would ever revisit, not knowing what is on the other side. My head tries to convince my heart that I have a choice, but my heart tells my head to shut the hell up.

I take a deep breath and click on the video. Soon Gwen's face appears, large on the screen, sitting up close to the lens. Her eyes are still filled with a deep sadness, and lines of grief remain etched across her face. Seeing her again is so bittersweet. My throat feels raw as tears blur my vision.

"Hi, Martin," she begins. "I should have contacted you before this. I should have found a way. I think I was hoping I had hurt you so deeply you had moved on and forgotten about me. But now I see that it's much worse. I've hurt you, but you can't get over it any more than I can. All I can say is I'm sorry, and hope you can forgive me."

"When Sebastian got sick I blamed myself. I felt it was my fault, that I was being punished for trying to be with you. I never felt I deserved to be happy, so this warped logic somehow made sense to me in my head. I became so desperate for him to get better, I thought pushing you away and going back to Tom would somehow fix everything. But it didn't. And then my whole world fell apart."

Gwen looks away from the screen. I can tell the years have not made the pain any easier to bear, as she takes a moment to gather herself back up.

"Tom and I didn't last very long after that. Once we cried out all our tears neither of us had any emotions left to give; certainly not any love. It was almost a year before we remembered why we could never make it work in the first place. After Tom and I separated again, I felt horrible and ashamed of what I put you through. When I found out you had enrolled in the Mars program I was sad, but also so proud of you. You made something come true for yourself that the rest of us can only dream of.

"I wish I could tell you to just forget about me but I know now that it isn't that simple. So instead, all I can say is that I'm here if you want to talk. I hope you do. I miss you. And yes, I still love you too. It seems like our whole lives we've loved each other from afar. Maybe that's just how it was always meant to be for us; out of synch and worlds apart."

"Goodbye, Martin. Hopefully just for now."

CHAPTER 13

Earth, 2022

I felt a cold drip of sweat run down my back as I smiled, trying not to look nervous. Across the table sat Dr. Lars, the chief psychologist for the Mars program. I had passed all of the earlier tests, but this was the biggest one yet. Already several candidates had been sent packing after only fifteen minutes of chatting with the good doctor. This felt like it was my "make or break" moment.

Dr. Lars appeared to have his own share of quirks. From the constant tapping of his cigarette stained fingers, to crops of erratic hair topping his heavyset features, he looked like a man who could recognize crazy from personal experience.

"Try and relax, Martin," Dr. Lars said with a quick smile that revealed crooked and yellowed teeth. "I need you to answer my questions truthfully. If you can do that, you have no reason to be nervous. Understand?"

I nodded even though I didn't believe him for a second.

"Good. Your file is very promising. Your background is an ideal fit for this program. It would seem that tragedy has uniquely shaped you for this purpose. While many may say they

72

are willing to leave everything they have ever known behind, what will be the truth once they do? And how will this truth change after five years? After ten years? After thirty?"

"If those are your questions, I'm afraid I don't know the answers," I replied.

Dr. Lars just laughed. "Ha! Very good. No, these are not my questions. You and my wife share the same eloquence in telling me to get to the point. So here it is."

He pushed a manila folder across the table to me. I opened it expecting to see a report about my earlier psychological tests, but instead I was surprised to find several photos of Gwen. They appeared to have been taken from afar without her knowing.

"I don't get it," I said truthfully. "What is this?"

"Surveillance photos," Dr. Lars replied. "With the considerable funds and resources being spent on this mission a most thorough background check was required for all of our finalists. The extraordinary nature of the mission means our efforts in investigating candidates must reflect the same level of vigor. We needed to know more about you than you know about yourself. We want to locate the cracks before they even form."

I realized I had been staring at the photos for too long, so I closed the folder and pushed it back across the table.

"There aren't any cracks here. Gwen is part of the past I left behind. I couldn't go back even if I wanted to, which I don't."

"Sometimes a bridge may not be as burned as it appears," said Dr. Lars. "What if I told you she and her husband divorced over a year ago?"

Opening the manila folder again, Dr. Lars leafed through the pictures and then turned and pushed it back towards me. I could see this time it was a photocopied document. A quick glance confirmed they were divorce papers with Gwen and Tom's names on them. My head began to swim as my heart pounded in my throat. It took all of my willpower to take slow deep breaths and remain calm.

But Dr. Lars wasn't finished yet.

"And what if I also told you that she has made several inquiries on your behalf? Your lady friend has been making efforts to track you down through your former contacts at the Canadian Space Agency. It would appear as though your past has not been left as far behind you as you might think."

"I see…" was all I managed to say through clenched teeth.

I was struggling with my emotions, but my efforts to conceal them weren't working, which made the situation even worse.

Dr. Lars sat there and watched me struggle, with a spark in his eye that told me he could read me like a book. Finally, he sat back in his chair, content with what he had seen.

"Martin, relax. Despite what you think, I am not here at this moment to judge you. If I didn't believe you had what it takes to make the voyage, we wouldn't even be having this conversation."

"Then why am I here?" I asked.

"That question is exactly the reason why you are here," Dr. Lars replied. He saw the confusion on my face, so he elaborated.

"Every candidate must ask themselves the question, 'why am I here?' Everyone thinks they know the answer when they first arrive, but they must look inside themselves before they will know the truth. Whatever you think you will gain in this will never equal all that you will lose. That loss will come back to haunt you in the form of guilt and regret. But in the end, it is up to you to decide if you want to live with this burden for the rest of your life. This is a decision that only you can make. But you must make it knowing all of the facts. So you see, it is not to me that you must tell the truth; it is to yourself."

Dr. Lars let his last statement hang in the air for a moment before continuing. "And so really I only have one question for you Martin, a most simple, and yet also a most difficult question as well."

"Which is?"

Dr. Lars leaned forward.

"Do you *really* want to go?"

CHAPTER 14

Mars, 2040

M artin, I am so sorry."

In my state of shock, the sound of Jomo's voice fades into the background as time and reality grinds to a halt around me. His presence in the room no longer registers.

The video message plays on repeat in my memory as I hope there is some way that I misunderstood. But no matter which way I reflect, the truth stares back.

I have cancer.

I hold the thought in my head, examining it, feeling the fear gnaw in from the edges the longer I force myself to take it in.

I am 50 years old and I am going to die from cancer, just like my mother.

No, probably not just like her.

She had been in a hospital bed, ravaged by the effects of chemotherapy and radiation. Over the last thirteen years the medical facilities in our little colony have improved, but it is still not equipped to deal with a disease like this. There are some drug therapies on-hand, and no doubt more would be shipped out on the next launch. The constant exposure to radiation was a risk we all knew could lead to this diagnosis. That, combined with years of inhaling my mother's second-hand smoke, and I was probably a ticking time bomb.

One of the important things I learned with my mother's cancer was that everyone used terms like "treatment" and "survival", but not "cure". Now I had heard the same phrase from the doctors at mission control:

"These treatments can potentially be very successful at extending the timeline for your survival."

But no mention of a "cure".

I remembered my mother lying in that hospital bed, her organs turned into poison, killing both malignant and healthy cells without discrimination. I already knew what "treatment" and "survival" looked like.

"I don't want any treatment," I finally say out loud.

"Martin, please," Jomo says, believing I had spoken to him, "You must."

I turn to look at my dear friend, the man who put the ghost of my brother to rest by stepping in to take his place. I can see the heartbreak etched on his face, but it is not enough.

"I'm sorry Jomo," I reply, "I can't."

"You saved my life when we first arrived here," Jomo pleads, "Please, give me time to try to save yours."

If sheer will was enough to cure my cancer, than I am certain that Jomo could find a way. I was always in awe at the depths of his determination. I hate being the one to disappoint him.

"Please understand Jomo," I reply, "The quality of the time I have left is more important to me now than the quantity."

"I won't give up on you," Jomo says. "I can't."

"I know. You never have."

It had begun as a nagging cough that had progressively become worse, which I tried to downplay until I started to cough up blood. Jomo stepped in and took control of the situation, collecting samples, sending test data back to Earth for consultation, and tirelessly researching every possibility.

I'm glad I asked him to join me while I received the results. The cancer was slow-moving, but had already begun to metastasize. The worst case scenario was two years; the best possible outcome was five. Despite living in a place where the environment outside my door could kill me in an instant, I had never felt so vulnerable.

I won't even have the honorable distinction of being the first Mars colonist to die on the planet. William had already stumbled his way into that historical footnote five years ago. He and Jesper spent their free time in pursuit of engineering the first-ever Martian beer. They eventually succeeded in creating a fine red ale with four times the normal alcoholic volume, which they cleverly dubbed "The Martian Masher".

William was entirely out of practice from his glory days at the local pub. After an evening of downing several pints of their brew, William decided he wanted to go experience the Martian landscape while still intoxicated. Unfortunately, he neglected to share his plan with any of the sober colonists who might have tried to talk him out of it or—at least—checked his gear before he went out.

An improper seal on his helmet poetically sealed William's fate. He was so drunk that he likely didn't notice he was suffocating. He was still walking away from the pod hatch when he collapsed. The rest of us were lucky he didn't leave the inner hatch open.

We buried William under a cairn of Martian rock not far from where he died. I suppose his tiny tomb will one day grow to become a monument for the settlers of the Mars colony; it's only a matter of time before history remembers him as a brave pioneer instead of a careless drunk.

Everyone gathered together in the main pod after the funeral. Looking at all of the faces, I was surprised at how many now I didn't even recognize. The community had grown from the tight group of team members I had trained with, to newcomers who hadn't even joined the program when Jomo and I arrived on Mars. For a few years many of these newcomers would make the pilgrimage after their arrival to come see me, and gush about how I had "inspired" them to make the same choice. I could never really be bothered to point out that just because they had made the same trip didn't mean they had made the same choice. Coming to join the colony now is a far cry from when Jomo and I established it. The generation of pioneers who built this colony is a different breed than the ones who now get to enjoy the fruits of all our labor. What annoys me the most is how much they all take it for granted.

It's no longer just about survival on the red planet; this new, younger group has arrived with even greater aspirations: terraforming. They have been experimenting with ways to use the remaining ice and moisture on the planet to affect the atmosphere, and the climate along with it. I know I won't live to see a day where humans might be able to venture outside without a helmet, but what I've seen so far makes me truly believe the day is coming.

There have even been whispers of the team back home working on a new technology designed to give us the ability to send colonists back to Earth. But by now, that news has little interest for me. Even if I were to live long enough for it to happen, my body would never be able to handle Earth's gravity. After decades of being acclimatized on Mars, having triple the force pressing down on me would make even the simple act of breathing intolerable. No, my journey to the red planet will end as it was always meant to be: as a one way trip.

What I remember the most about William's memorial was how resolute it made me feel that I didn't want the same send-off when it was my turn. I didn't want to become another pile of rocks in our Martian graveyard, a background photo op for every future visitor and tourist.

I wanted something different. I wanted to be cremated and have my ashes scattered into one of the Martian windstorms. I wanted a chance to once again become stardust.

Of course I had no idea how it would be possible. We

didn't have any sort of crematorium, and open flame was something to be avoided with extreme prejudice in our delicate, pressurized habitat.

I know that once Jomo accepts the futility of my situation, he will help me with my final wish. He is the only one now who understands why this means so much to me. He understands the pull of the stars on my soul.

Perhaps Gwen would also have understood, but I burned that bridge a long time ago. Even with my diagnosis, there was no way I would try to contact her. I had already said goodbye, and I had meant it. Although thinking about it always carried the same sadness, it was tempered with relief knowing it had been the right thing to do—for her sake.

I couldn't bear to see her make the worst mistake of her life.

CHAPTER 15

Mars, 2037

I've gone and done it, Martin," Gwen said on the recording. She held her tablet with both arms crossed over her chest, the screen turned outwards for me to see the display.

"I've applied for the Mars program. I know you don't think I should come. I know you have your own regrets about leaving, but there's nothing here for me anymore. I feel like I'm asleep, and all I dream about is Mars. I want to wake up and remember what it feels like to be alive. I want to wake up and be with you, Martin. We keep letting things get between us and keep us apart. Why let a little thing like being on separate planets stand in our way? I don't want us to have to keep sending video messages millions of miles across the galaxy. I want to talk to you—to really talk to you. When only one person talks, there's a lot that can't be said."

Gwen lifted her eyes and looked into the lens, across an endless void, and right through me.

"I love you, Martin. I always have. I always will. It's not too late for us. At least it's not too late for me. I hope it's not too late for you. See you… later."

The video came to an end and I felt the same conflict of emotions waging war inside of me. The thought of us being together made me feel euphoric, but the cost that she would have to pay made me feel terrible. She was chasing a fantasy as much as I was. I knew I could never live up to that sort of expectation. How could I ask her to sacrifice her whole world for me when I had never told her the whole truth?

I agonized for days over what to say. I tried to think of a way to explain things so that she would stay away without going away. But in the end, I had to admit to myself doing so would just continue a lifetime of heartbreak. It was time to face reality and make a clean break for the both of us.

I tapped the record icon on my screen and sat back to compose my thoughts. The usual quiet hum of machinery in my pod now sounded very loud. I tried to remind myself that this was just a recording, but my heart was pounding and my face felt flush. I took a deep breath to try to steady my racing pulse, and launched right into it.

"Hi Gwen… You're right. You shouldn't come. I don't want you to come. You said we keep letting things get between us, but the truth is that I didn't just let this happen, I made this happen. I knew about your divorce before I left. I even knew that you came looking for me. I could have made the choice to stay and we could have been together right now, living the life we talked about all those years ago during our summer in Montreal. Maybe I would have had the guts to ask you to marry me. Maybe you would have been crazy enough to say yes."

Before I can put the next thought into words I'm betrayed by a stream of tears running down my face. I have to wipe them away and clear my throat before continuing.

"Maybe… we would have had a kid or two of our own. I know I never said this to you before, and I know it's not fair for me to tell you this now—but I always wanted kids. I wanted to have kids with you. An then, after Sebastian… I knew there was no way you could ever replace him and I couldn't ask you to risk that kind of devastation again. I thought the past meant that there was no future for us. If I couldn't have a family with you, I didn't want to live on the planet anymore.

"But I was an idiot, Gwen. You're the bravest person I've ever known. You might not have said yes. But then again, maybe you would've. I should have at least given you a choice. It was the worst mistake of my life and I'll regret it for the rest of my life. I'm so, so sorry.

"You said you hoped it wasn't too late for me, but once I made that choice, I think it was too late for both of us. I will always miss you, but you giving up everything to come here because we should be together is a lie. I did this to us. I am responsible. And I am sorry for everything I have put you through. I can't allow you to throw your life away for me. Besides, you don't understand what it really means to live here.

"You live on a beautiful blue planet where you can walk outside and feel the warmth of the sun on your face, the wind on your skin, or even catch snowflakes on your tongue. There are none of those things here. I live in a can, surrounded by rocks and dust, breathing stale manufactured air, with a million ways to die at every turn.

"Yes, it has been an incredible experience to come here, and to have done the things I've done. But now, I'm done. I'm homesick. I want to go home. I've wanted to go home for a very long time. But I know I never will. I know I will never see Earth again. I can't even begin to describe to you how terrible it feels, knowing this. We don't belong here—none of us do. We are all aliens on this planet, with no way home."

"Please, don't make the same mistake. Appreciate the world around you. It may be all you've ever known, but when it's a distant blue speck in the sky, you'll be amazed at how lucky you were to have been a part of it."

"Gwen, please… Go live your life. Make new dreams. Forget about me. You deserve better. You always have. Goodbye, Gwen."

I tapped the screen to stop the recording, and then exhaled.

I felt light-headed.

Empty.

I wept until my body shook.

Gwen never sent a reply. Even after a few months I still held out some hope that I might log in and find a message from her. But after more than two years, I had to admit that she was gone forever. It was a strange feeling to have accomplished exactly what you set out to do, despite it being the exact opposite of what you wanted.

The very definition of a hollow victory.

And yet, the most important thing was not about how I felt, it was about Gwen. It was about saving her. It was about saving her from me.

But without *her*, there was no longer anyone who could save *me*.

CHAPTER 16

Mars, 2042

Some days the pain is so bad I want to lie down and never get back up again. On those days, I think back to the little boy who used to look up and dream of living among the stars. That little boy reminds me my dream has come true and to remember how truly lucky I am. The pain is there to remind me that I am still alive. Then the little boy tells me to stop feeling sorry for myself and get on my feet.

It's been a year since my diagnosis, and I can feel the cancer slowly eating away at me. It has spread out from my chest and latched on to other parts of my body, sending ripples of pain along my nerves like a plucked string. Jomo is always offering me something for the pain, but I refuse because the thing I fear the most is losing control of my mind. I've spent too much of my life trying to escape, it's time I stand my ground and stare the end down as it rushes towards me. At the very least I don't want to accidentally go stumbling outside and leave an airlock open.

Jomo has come up with a solution for my final wishes, with the help of Jesper and a little research. Once I die, they will treat my remains with a process known as Alkaline Hydrolysis, where lye will be used together with heat and pressure to dissolve my body into liquid and bone in a matter of a few hours. The remaining bones will be so fragile that they can be easily crushed into ash by hand and scattered into the wind. Although the details are a little gruesome, I still find the end result comforting. It is nice to know my atoms will be leaving this place, joining the dust storms to roam the red planet for eternity.

When Jomo knocks and enters my pod, I immediately notice an unusual smile on his face.

"I don't suppose that smile means you've discovered the cure for cancer, does it?" I ask.

"Something even more remarkable, I think," Jomo replies. "Come with me, this is something you have to see for yourself."

I want to protest, but there's something about the look in Jomo's eye that makes me stand up and shuffle after him.

Recently, I've been less inclined to venture out of my pod, but when I do I'm always amazed at how large the colony has become. A few interconnected pods have grown into a sprawling facility, with a maze of corridors and even some large open rooms.

The sick bay has also developed into a sophisticated medical center, with facilities and equipment worthy of Jomo and his growing staff.

When we arrive, I'm surprised to find the sick bay processing a new group of arrivals. Further proof at how out of the loop I've become. It's hard to believe there was once a time when I knew the exact number of days before a new crew would arrive. Now I can't even tell our population has increased until I notice the new faces.

"When did they get in?" I ask Jomo.

"A few hours ago," Jomo replies. "Some of them even claim they remember who the two of us are."

"They probably remember you more than me. Nobody even bothers to correct the death hoaxes anymore. Everyone just assumes I'm dead already."

I see Jomo's smile suddenly blossom into a goofy grin, but his eyes are looking over my shoulder.

"Not everyone," he says.

"Martin?"

I turn and see one of the new astronauts rising unsteadily to their feet.

I feel my heart tighten in my chest.

Gwen.

My first thought is that I'm imagining her. I'm seeing her face on someone else. It's a trick of the light. The cancer has spread to my brain and I'm having a delusion. There's no way this can be real. There's no way she can be here.

Gwen sees the look in my eyes and breaks the silence.

"It's me. I'm here. I'm really here."

I try to speak, but I feel like all of the air has been sucked out of the room.

"But… I… No…"

She crosses the remaining distance between us in an instant and kisses me. I crush her into me and she squeezes back. The pain that has wracked my body for months now seems distant and unimportant.

I feel time slow down in this perfect moment, as though everyone around us, the planet—the rest of existence—all of it has left us behind. Then I realize I'm weeping and my body is shaking. I look at Gwen's beautiful face and see her tears mirror mine. We stare at each other and just continue to cry without saying a word.

Finally, my legs begin to buckle from the strain and Gwen has to help me over to a chair before I collapse. Even in my emaciated state, I can feel her struggling under my weight. I am reminded of the physical toll she has paid having travelled over half a year though space to get here. Yet somehow, she seems almost superhuman compared to me.

"I didn't want you to come…" I gasp as I sit.

"I know," Gwen replies. "But I came anyway. This was my

dream first, remember? Becoming an astronaut was my idea. You just stole it from me. This was just as much about my dreams as it was about seeing you. Coming here was my decision, and no one tells me what I can or cannot do."

"When I didn't hear back from you…"

"You were never going to change my mind, so I decided not to give you the chance. The years of training in isolation took care of the rest."

"But you don't understand!" I say. "Now it's so much worse. You've come all this way, and I'm—"

"I know," Gwen replies. "That's how I got moved up the ranks to come here so quickly."

"But you've given up too much! There's no way back for you now…!"

Gwen kneels down and takes my hands in her own. Through my bleary eyes, the light glows behind her head and I am struck with the first memory I have of her; an angel emerging from the darkness.

"You still don't get it, do you?" Gwen says. "I love you. And I know you love me. That's it. Nothing else matters. I came here knowing exactly what I was leaving behind, just like you did. We've both had a lifetime of loss. It's time we took back something for ourselves.

"I would rather give up everything to spend our last few days together, than to go the rest of my life being apart from you."

She is crying again, and seeing her in front of me, in the flesh, looking so beautiful and so perfect, the only thing I can think of is to kiss her again.

This time I can feel my heart pounding as the blood pulses though my body. It's been a long time since I've had something other than pain to remind me that I'm alive. But this bag of bones isn't dead yet, not if I have anything to say about it. I will claw and bite and drag this broken body forward through every moment I have left. I will make time work for us. I will turn every minute I get from now on into a lifetime. I owe her at least that much.

"There's something else you have to see," Gwen says once we finally regain our composure. "Something amazing I saw on my way in."

"Okay," I reply.

"First you're going to need to suit up."

"We're going outside? What is it?" I ask.

"Something to prove to you once and for all that the universe wants us to be together." Gwen replies.

As she helps me with my space suit, I'm that nine-year-old boy again, breathless and excited in her presence, ready to follow her anywhere.

We make our way to the main airlock and fix on our helmets. She checks my equipment seals and asks me to do the same for her. As I watch Gwen in this surreal moment, feeling like I'm outside of my body, I can't help but be impressed and proud of her skills as an astronaut. It's an amazing transformative moment, seeing someone you've known for your entire life, finally becoming what they were always meant to be.

Gwen the astronaut.

She is magnificent.

We hold hands like a pair of high school lovers as she closes the inner hatch and equalizes the atmosphere between the two environments. I help her open the outer hatch and we step out together into the dim Martian morning. It has been a long time since I have taken a walk outside of the habitat, but with Gwen at my side it feels like I am experiencing the breathtaking vista for the first time.

I notice there are several other colonists already outside. Many are jumping around like little excited children. I look over at Gwen and she sees the confusion on my face through my helmet. But she doesn't say a word. Instead, she just looks up.

I follow her gaze, expecting to spot something in the distant sky. It takes a moment to focus my attention on what is all around me.

At first I had just dismissed the debris falling around us as heavy dust particles. But when I take a closer look I can't believe my eyes.

Snow.

Falling all around us… is snow.

I hold out my hand and see the gray flakes settling on my palm.

"Snow…! I'd heard it was possible with the increased levels of methane in the atmosphere from the terraforming, but in all the decades we've been here we've never…" I am too astonished to finish.

Gwen takes my other hand in hers and turns to face me, pressing her face shield against mine.

"Just like a million stars, falling from the sky, wouldn't you say?" Gwen asks.

Her voice brings the memory of our first meeting back to me, across a galaxy of space and time.

"It's the most beautiful thing I've ever seen," I reply. Then I look at her.

"—Almost."

Gwen smiles.

Together at last, we stand on the planet Mars, under the stars and snowflakes, feeling the stardust inside both of us calling out to the vast universe beyond.

And for the first time in a lifetime, I finally get that feeling.

I am home.

ABOUT THE AUTHOR

Stephen M. Braund has spent the last decade as a senior writer and game designer for Ganz Studios, where he helped create the pop culture hit "Webkinz", a multiplayer online world for kids. Previously, he has worked as a screenwriter and producer in the Canadian film industry. He currently lives north of Toronto with his wife Christine and their two sons.

stephenmbraund.com
Twitter: @stephenmbraund

Also by Stephen M. Braund:

A Bitter Pill (short story)

The Little Robot (short story)

www.ingramcontent.com/pod-product-compliance
Lightning Source LLC
Chambersburg PA
CBHW070639130626
46555CB00006B/2610